LESSONS
IN
LOVE

LESSONS
IN
LOVE

•

Debby Mayne

AVALON BOOKS
NEW YORK

PRINTED IN THE UNITED STATES OF AMERICA
ON ACID-FREE PAPER
BY HADDON CRAFTSMEN, BLOOMSBURG, PENNSYLVANIA

This book is dedicated to the loving memory of my mother June and my two grandmothers Hazel and Maxine, all strong women who showed me that I can accomplish goals by working hard and never giving up.

I'm especially grateful to my husband Wally and my daughters Alison and Lauren for their encouragement. Without them, I'd be lost. Thanks to my friends and fellow romance authors Kim and Kathy, I have a book that someone wanted to buy. I'd also like to thank my BG buddies Denise, Connie, Tina, Gail, Lynda, Stephanie, Amy, Terri, Phyllis, LaRita, Cindi, Patty, Carole, and Jodi for hanging out with me for so long and being my biggest cheerleaders. Editors Erin Cartwright and Philip Harley gave me the encouragement to continue trying, and I did. All these people had faith in me and without them, it would have been impossible.

Chapter One

Stephanie backed out of her classroom, smiling at the children she was leaving in the care of Mr. Phillips, the principal. "I won't be long."

Mr. Phillips smiled back at her. "Take your time, Miss Mansfield. This picture will be in the yearbook, and since this is the first time we've ever had one at the elementary grade level, I want everyone to look their best."

Slowly, Stephanie nodded. She didn't want to tell him what was on her mind—that she wasn't the least bit photogenic—so she kept her mouth shut.

"Hey, Steph," Marla Sawyer, the teacher in the class next to Stephanie's said as she joined her in the hallway. "Isn't it exciting to have someone like Nathan Holloway doing our pictures?"

1

Rolling her eyes, Stephanie shrugged. "A thrill I could do without."

"Oh, come on, Steph. Lighten up. I've seen some of his work, and it's really, really good."

The clickety-clack of their heels echoed through the tiled hallways of the old school Stephanie Mansfield had attended when she was a little girl. She took a deep breath and allowed the blended smells of chalk, small children, and cafeteria food to enter her nostrils.

School was the place Stephanie felt most comfortable. She loved everything about the atmosphere, all the way from writing on the chalkboard to the comfort she found in its very existence. She felt safe there.

Marla cleared her throat as they got closer to the empty classroom that had been designated as the photo studio for Nathan Holloway. Mr. Phillips had gone to college with the famous New York photographer, and they were roommates during their last year there. And for some odd reason that Stephanie couldn't understand, Mr. Phillips had talked Nathan into doing the staff pictures for this yearbook, something she wished had never come up.

Whoever heard of an elementary school having a yearbook, anyway? Wasn't that something to look forward to in high school?

While all the other teachers loved the idea, and the children certainly didn't argue, Stephanie just sat there wishing she could find an excuse not to be included.

It was bad enough to have the big nose and eyes that were set too wide. And her lips. They were much too full, so when she smiled, it looked like she could fit a whole plate of food in her mouth without having to cut it into small bites. Why did she have to have her picture taken so people could gawk at her awkward features whenever they felt like it?

"Come on in," the school secretary said from her post at the door. "Mr. Holloway's been waiting for you."

Stephanie gulped and held back to let Marla go first. Maybe he'd run out of film, and she'd have to sacrifice having her picture being included.

"Don't be shy," the secretary said. Then she nodded to Marla and said, "Why don't you go first?"

Stephanie stood back and watched Marla go to the other side of the room, her hands up around her hair, patting it down on her head, acting like she could actually make a difference now. Marla was pretty, though, so it really didn't matter.

It took about five minutes for Marla to have her picture taken in several different poses. "Now it's your turn," the school secretary said, pulling her by the arm and leading her toward the place that had been set up on the other side of the curtain.

Stephanie had never seen Nathan Holloway, but she'd seen his pictures, which just happened to be on practically every billboard that featured the most beautiful cosmetics and fashion models in the world. She still didn't see him. He was hidden behind the camera, with only his arm within view.

"Have a seat, and I'll be with you in just a minute. I've got a few lighting adjustments to make before we continue. The sun's changing position."

Stephanie did as she was told. Hopefully, the sun would go into an eclipse, and he'd have to cancel the rest of the pictures.

After what seemed like an eternity to Stephanie, the man behind the camera moved and came toward her. Suddenly, her mouth went dry, and her hands began to shake.

This guy had the most incredible blue eyes she'd ever seen in her life. Not just your everyday-garden-variety-type blue. They were the color of the deepest part of the ocean when standing on the highest cliff, looking down. Their color was further enhanced by the dark, bushy eyebrows that formed a frame over them, and his jaw that provided the strength of character in his face.

And he actually smiled at her. Her heart did a double flip.

"Your name?" he asked softly.

"My name?" For a moment, Stephanie's mind drew a blank, and she couldn't even think of her name, let alone answer the photographer.

"Yes, your name. Mrs. . . ." he said, gesturing for her to finish his sentence.

"Oh," she said. "I'm not married," she answered with a self-satisfied smile.

"That's nice to know," he replied, shaking his head. "But I still need a name."

Stephanie felt like kicking herself for this one. *What an idiot I am!* Nathan Holloway could care less if she was married, divorced, widowed, or all of the above. He just needed a name to go with the picture.

"Sorry," she said as she hung her head. "Mansfield. Stephanie Mansfield."

He nodded once, his eyebrows raised. "Okay, Stephanie Mansfield, let's see what angle we need to give you your best shot."

Suddenly, panic rose in Stephanie's throat. There was no way to hide her nose and huge lips from the camera. Not if she faced it, anyway.

But she couldn't speak. She just sat there and let him tilt her head to one side, then to the other. The warmth radiating from his fingertips counteracted the shivers the gaze from his blue eyes sent down her spine. His hands remained gentle as he tried different poses before settling on one he seemed satisfied with.

"Hold that for a moment, Stephanie," he said as he walked back behind the camera. She felt like jumping up and following him. But she just sat there, her muscles stiff.

Naturally, her ankle started to itch, but Stephanie froze in the position he'd placed her. She didn't dare move to scratch.

"What?" he said as he popped his head from behind the camera.

Puzzled, Stephanie narrowed her eyes. "Why did you say 'what'?"

"You look like someone just put ants in your pants," he said with a frown.

"My leg itches." How did he know that?

"Then scratch it." Nathan let out an exasperated sigh. "I'll wait."

Stephanie reached down and rubbed her ankle that had miraculously stopped itching. Then she smiled back at him. "I'm ready now."

He snorted with his eyes closed, which was good. That way she didn't have to look at them. It was hard to concentrate around this man, something Stephanie wasn't used to. "Get back into position."

She tried. She really did. In fact, if Nathan hadn't crossed the room in three long strides and tilted her head back to the side, she would have sworn that she was in the exact same position he'd placed her in just a moment ago.

"Okay, now hold it," he said, returning to the camera.

Right when he snapped the picture, Stephanie felt it coming on. A hiccup! It had to be because she was nervous. All this itching and moving around reminded her of the children she taught all day.

"What now?" he asked as he jumped back around to the front of the camera.

Stephanie reached up and covered her mouth with her hand. "I've got hiccups."

"Hiccups?"

Nodding, she repeated, "Hiccups."

"Then do something to stop it."

"I'll have to get some water." She just sat there and waited for him to release her.

He began to wave his arms around. "Then do it." He raked his fingers through his hair and slapped his thigh in one fluid motion. "I haven't got all day."

Stephanie could hear the exasperation in his voice, and she felt awful about holding him up. Really, she did. But she couldn't help it if she suddenly got the hiccups. Well, could she?

Stephanie Mansfield—Miss Mansfield—had a charisma he was used to from the models in New York. But she obviously was unaware of it. He had to admit, she was much better off not knowing.

Nathan stood there and watched her get up and walk out the door of the classroom Ed Phillips had set up for him. Never in a million years had he ever imagined himself photographing schoolteachers in an old school that reminded him of his own failures as a child. He'd never done well in reading, writing, and 'rithmetic. But he'd been a great photographer, ever since his uncle had given him his first camera when he turned ten.

It had taken him all of about an hour to figure out how to use the thing, and then he'd begun the first of what turned out to be his life's passion. Photography.

He'd managed to get through high school with passing grades, then when he went to college, he was lucky enough to room with Ed Phillips, who tutored him in exchange for doing all his photography when he needed projects. It was a fair exchange, and Nathan had been grateful, thinking he'd actually gotten the better end of the deal. In fact, he'd told Ed this and made the offer that if he ever wanted anything in the future, to just call.

And Ed had. He'd called him with excitement about this new project he'd decided to take on for the school. Since a yearbook had never been done at this grade level in Hartsville, Ed wanted Nathan to be the first photographer. It had to be good, and he knew that with Nathan's skill, it would be the best.

What could Nathan have said but yes? Of course he'd come to Hartsville and take pictures of the teachers. How hard could that be? He'd fly down for a few days, visit with Ed, drop by the school with his camera, and then head on back to his life in New York.

His life in the studio. His life of snapping pictures of the most beautiful models in the world. His life of going home to an empty apartment each day after work. His life of loneliness.

Nathan sighed as he waited for Stephanie Mansfield to return. Loneliness was a state of mind, he told himself. Mind over matter, he added. It was time to snap out of this mood and play the big-shot photographer.

By the time Stephanie returned, Nathan felt a little better. In fact, he actually enjoyed looking at the fresh face of this woman who had such unusual features that made her look more like an exotic model than a schoolteacher.

He'd never had a schoolteacher who looked like Miss Mansfield. If he had, he might have made much better grades. She elicited a strange combination of warmth, comfort, and fascination in him.

"Feeling better?" he asked as she sat back down in the chair he'd draped with black fabric. He knew he needed to be gentle with this one.

She nodded. "Much."

"Okay, now you need to try to remember the pose I showed you."

"How's this?" she asked, tilting her head and smiling at him, softly and naturally.

"Perfect," he said as he stepped behind the camera and snapped her picture before she had a chance to move. "Now let's try another one."

He moved her around and snapped a half dozen pictures of this gorgeous teacher. He'd only taken two or three of each of the rest of the staff, but Stephanie Mansfield was different. And he'd never been able to resist a beautiful model when it came to taking her picture.

"How about a few motion shots?" he asked when he finished the posed ones of her in the chair.

"Motion shots?" she asked innocently.

Oh man, she wasn't in the business. She didn't have a clue what he was talking about.

"Motion shots," he said softly as he took her hands in his. "You move, and I follow you around with the camera and take shots in different positions."

"D-do we have time?" she asked. "I've heard that you're on a tight schedule."

Nathan glanced down at his watch. He'd already spent way too much time with this teacher, and he still had more than half the faculty to go.

With a deep sigh, he nodded. "You're right. I have to finish up with the staff."

She chewed on her bottom lip, obviously thinking about something she wanted to say. But she didn't. She just backed out of the room and said, "Thank you, Mr. Holloway. It was a lot more fun than I thought it would be."

Nathan smiled to himself. Miss Mansfield was the first female teacher he'd shot today who didn't try to put on her best imitation of what she thought a New

York model would be. In fact, one of the women had actually asked him what her chances were of being discovered. After she coquettishly tossed her too-long hair over her shoulder and batted her eyelashes at him one time too many.

When Miss Mansfield walked into the room, he had the feeling that she didn't want to be there. And that intrigued him.

He took pictures of another half dozen teachers before Ed Phillips came to let him know it was time for lunch. Nathan tossed his paperwork on the table and dropped the black cover over the camera.

"It's been quite some time since I've had a school lunch," Nathan said as he followed his friend to the door.

"Oh, I don't expect you to eat school cafeteria food," Ed said, shaking his head.

"What else am I going to get in this fabulous institution?"

Ed pointed down the street, toward the small shopping district in town. "We have a pretty good diner I thought you might like to try. It's not New York, but it's the best we've got. That is," he added, "if you're up for a little home cooking."

"Home cooking, huh?" Nathan said. "It's been a long time since I've had that."

"That's what I thought," Ed mentioned. "I just hope your belt has a looser notch. They have the best coconut cream pie you've ever tasted."

"I don't remember *ever* having coconut cream pie."

"Then you're in for a treat."

Since it was such a beautiful day, they walked. Nothing was far in this town, and that intrigued Nathan. Most of the places he went in New York required using some sort of transportation, whether he rode the subway or took a cab. This was refreshing for a change, but he couldn't imagine making a habit of it.

The diner had no menus, just a blackboard hanging on the wall, with the daily specials scribbled beside one price. Nathan chuckled.

"They only have three dishes?" he asked.

Ed shook his head. "No, that's just the specials. Locals know their menu by heart, so they don't bother putting it on the tables. If you need one, I can ask Cissy."

"Cissy?"

"The waitress," Ed said as he made his way toward a booth in the back by the window.

Cissy seemed to sense when they were ready. She showed up at the table with a pad in one hand and a pen poised in the other. "Special today, Ed?"

Ed glanced at Nathan, who pondered the chalkboard. "How's the meat loaf?" Nathan asked.

Cissy's eyes lit up. "That's my favorite thing we serve. We use only the best ground chuck and season it with salt and pepper. Then it's topped with ketchup and baked for an hour."

"Ketchup, huh?" Nathan said. This definitely wasn't New York. But what the heck? "Then I'll take the meat loaf."

Cissy was more pleased with his selection than she probably should have been, but that was okay. Nathan was happy to make her day if that was all it took.

"Ed?" she said, turning to the other man.

"Same," he replied, a closed-mouth grin on his lips. As soon as Cissy was gone, he looked at Nathan. "Well, how'd it go this morning?"

Nathan shrugged. "Fine. This really isn't a hard job, you know. In fact, most of your teachers are more cooperative than most of the models I work with."

"We have some real beauties here in Hartsville, don't we?" Ed asked, pride written all over his face.

"They've got potential," Nathan said, sidestepping the obvious. He could tell that his friend loved this town, and he wasn't going to put it down, just because he was used to more. Besides, no matter how much Ed tried to sell the place, Nathan wasn't buying.

"Did you get a load of Miss Pritchett, the kindergarten teacher?" Ed asked.

Nathan had to dig deep to remember someone by

that name. But when he did, an image of a woman with bleached blond hair and exaggerated curves came to mind. "Oh, yes, I remember her."

"Nice-looking, huh?"

How should he put this? The last thing Nathan wanted to do was make a negative comment about his friend's taste in women. "Someone you're interested in, Ed?"

Ed mumbled something and shook his head. "I would be if I could get away with it. It's not a good policy to date people who work for you."

"Why not? I do it all the time." Nathan picked up the tray of crackers and studied them for a moment before putting it back down on the table.

"I'll bet you do," Ed said, his eyes lighting up with delight. "Tell me about it."

Shrugging, Nathan said, "What do you want to know?"

Ed leaned forward like a little boy eager to inspect the goods at the candy counter. "What's it like, Nathan, to be surrounded by gorgeous women all day?"

"You get used to it after a while. They start to look alike."

"I don't know if I could take it. I'd probably have a heart attack with so many of them, day in and day out."

Day in and day out. Yeah, that's what it was. Beautiful women flocking to his studio, only to leave in a state of exhaustion after hours of shooting pictures, posing, and pouting their lips, fans blowing their tresses, makeup artists stopping the session every few minutes to retouch their faces. It grew old, but it was a good job. At least Nathan did well. And he was grateful. It allowed him to live in one of the nicest apartments in Manhattan.

Several people stopped at the booth and spoke with Ed, who in turn introduced Nathan. Everyone seemed impressed by the fact that he lived in New York. He just smiled and answered their questions.

Finally, after he ate his oversalted meat loaf that was swimming in a pool of ketchup, he started to fold his napkin and put it on the table. Ed shook his head. "Not yet, Nathan. You've got to try the coconut cream pie."

"I don't know if I could eat another bite," Nathan argued.

"But you have to. This place is known for their desserts."

Ed had twisted his arm. He didn't have a choice that he could see. Oh well, at least it gave him more time to talk about his work and find out about the one person Ed hadn't brought up.

As soon as Cissy took their order, Nathan began to fidget with the corner of his napkin. "How long has Stephanie Mansfield been a teacher at your school?" he asked as nonchalantly as he could.

"Miss Mansfield?" Ed said, obviously stunned that Nathan would bring up her name. "Let's see." He looked up at the ceiling and thought for a moment. "Three years, maybe?"

"She seems like she'd be a good teacher."

"That she is," Ed said, nodding. "It's a good thing, too, because I doubt she'll ever get married."

Nathan laughed out loud. That was the most ridiculous thing he'd ever heard. How would Ed even pretend to know something like that? "What makes you say that?"

"Look at her!" Ed said. "She gives men the impression she's not interested, and she's not exactly the prettiest thing in the world."

Chapter Two

Nathan was stunned. "What? I can't believe you just said that, Ed."

"Well, it's true," Ed said sheepishly.

"You still have no way of knowing what the future holds for other people." Stephanie's image was in the forefront of Nathan's mind, and from what he remembered, she was the most attractive woman in the school. At least, to him she was.

"No, that's true," Ed agreed. "But I would be willing to put a bigger wager on Miss Pritchett."

"She's overprocessed," Nathan said as he picked up his water glass and fished for a piece of ice.

"Haven't you heard the saying, 'Gentlemen prefer blondes'?" Ed said, chuckling.

"This gentleman doesn't."

Nathan studied Ed uncomfortably shuffling his napkin around on the table. He wasn't ready for the steady glare when Ed looked directly at him and said, "So you're interested in Miss Mansfield?"

Nothing like being direct. "Interested? Well, not exactly interested, although I did find her attractive."

"And you don't feel that way about Miss Pritchett?"

"No."

A low chuckle came from Ed's throat. "Different strokes, I suppose."

"Yeah," Nathan replied. "Different strokes."

"Whaddya think about the pie? Good, huh?" Ed changed the subject so abruptly, Nathan had to shift mental gears.

"Yes, very good." How could he tell him what he really thought, that the pie was nothing but a bunch of overripe bananas topped with instant pudding and way too much whipped cream? He couldn't. "Very good," he repeated, almost as much to convince himself as to keep his friend from getting his feelings hurt.

Ed was obviously proud of his little town. No sense in embarrassing him.

"Ready to get back to the grindstone?" Ed said as he stood up and thrust his hand into his pocket, extracting a wallet.

"Sure." He reached for the check.

"Oh, no you don't," Ed said, snapping it from Nathan's hand. "This is on me."

"Thanks." Nathan's stomach already hurt, and he wondered if he'd be able to make it through the afternoon. At least he'd done the majority of his work that morning, so he only had a few stragglers left.

"I think the teachers are really enjoying having you here. It gives them a chance to get a feel for what it's like to be a model," Ed said as he opened the heavy school door.

Once again, Nathan kept his mouth shut. Posing for school pictures was nothing like being a model, which entailed grueling hours of holding a position, having people poke and prod at the hair, the face, and the body, never mind the discomfort of having to don clothes out of season.

"Looks like you have your social schedule filled while you're in town, Nathan," Ed said when they opened the classroom door and found slips of paper and cards that had been slipped beneath the door. "At least, you do if you want to."

Nathan shrugged. He stepped over the amateur portfolios and flowery notes to get to his equipment. It had to be adjusted for the afternoon sun. "I brought some work with me, so I doubt I'll have time to do much socializing."

"Suit yourself," Ed took a few steps toward the door, still scrutinizing Nathan. "But most men would be in hog heaven in your shoes."

As soon as Ed was gone, Nathan glanced at his watch. Good. He still had fifteen minutes before the next teacher was scheduled to arrive. That gave him a chance to recover from the high-cholesterol lunch Ed seemed to enjoy so much.

Nathan fidgeted with his camera, adjusting it for light, then for distance. He moved the chair where the teachers sat to make sure he got everything in the right place for the position of the sun.

Over the years, Nathan had photographed more people than he could count. There were young ones, middle-aged ones, and a few elderly ones when the client needed to sell something to the senior set. Most of the time, the people were professionals, and by the time he'd gotten to them, they'd become jaded. They knew the ropes. They came in, did what they had to do, then they left.

But this was different. The teachers here, mostly women, all seemed to be under the impression that they might have a shot at the big time. All except one woman, that is. Stephanie Mansfield. And she was the most likely person in this entire school to actually have any success at all in modeling.

Just the thought of Miss Pritchett trying to make it in New York elicited a smile from Nathan. Ed Phillips definitely had a different idea of photogenic than he had. Too bad Ed didn't feel free to date whomever he wanted, because Nathan sensed that Miss Pritchett might be perfect for Ed.

Nathan was startled by the school secretary when she finally arrived at the door. "Ready for your next subject, Mr. Holloway?"

"Sure," he said after he straightened up. "Send the next one in."

There were only a few left for that day, so Nathan knew he could get back to his hotel before the sun set. Even though he chose to live in the big city, he still loved photographing the sunset out in the open country. There was nothing like capturing the image of the bright yellow ball of fire as it transformed the sky around it to oranges, reds, and in some cases pinks and purples. In fact, it was breathtaking.

Since the school seemed like a safe place to leave his equipment, Nathan chose not to break down the studio. He had to come back tomorrow. All he took when he left was his camera, which he would never leave anywhere.

He'd almost made it to his rental car when he heard Ed's voice. "Hey, Nathan, I was hoping I could catch you before you leave. I'm having a few people over tonight, and I was wondering if you could make it."

"Uh, well . . ." Nathan began.

Ed had caught up with him and looked at him earnestly. "And I have to admit, I told everyone you'd be there. In fact, it's in your honor."

In spite of his minor irritation, Nathan snickered. "I'm not dead yet, Ed."

His hands thrust deeply in his pockets, Ed looked at him with hope. "You *can* make it, can't you?"

Nathan let out the breath he was holding and nodded. "Sure. I'll be there. Just tell me what time to show up and what to bring."

As soon as Nathan had the information, he took off. He never should have let Ed talk him into coming to Hartsville, but how could he have turned down someone who stroked his ego like Ed had? Besides, he'd needed a change of scenery after that last two-month photo shoot for *Boomerang!*, the trendiest of all the teen magazines. Two months of a steady diet of egocentric teens was enough to drive anyone batty. The guys were constantly hitting on the girls, who squealed whenever they did that. And then they griped nonstop whenever the guys didn't pay any attention to them. Was he ever that young?

Nathan headed west and drove all the way through town. He wasn't about to miss the sunset, even if it meant getting there hours beforehand.

On the way, he stopped at a small grocery store and picked up a few items for a solitary picnic. The good thing about doing that was that he could get whatever he wanted without having to think about pleasing someone else.

Now that was a novel concept. Not having to think about pleasing someone else with models and moody assistants around him all day long was something he wasn't used to.

He got in his car and kept on heading west. The drive was pretty and picturesque. He went for about ten minutes before he figured he'd better find a spot or risk disappointing his friend by not being at the party. Finally, he decided to pull off on a dirt road that led to a patch of trees. Hopefully, there would be a place for him to sit and just enjoy the show when the sun dropped below the horizon.

What he got at the end of the dirt road was much more than he'd bargained for. There, on the other side of the trees, in the middle of a deep clearing, was a tiny white house that appeared to be well-kept and lived in. Hopefully, the inhabitant wouldn't mind him intruding.

Better stop and ask, he thought. No sense alarming anyone. Out here, being this close to someone's house was trespassing.

He went up to the door and knocked. No one answered. There were no sounds coming from the house. He went over to the window a few feet from the front door and peeked in. It was dark.

After letting out a sigh of relief, Nathan went back to his car, gathered up a few things—his groceries, his camera, and the blanket he'd brought from the hotel—and carried them to the other side of the trees. He didn't feel like moving his car.

Within an hour, the sun had moved into a position that had begun changing the sky noticeably. He snapped one picture at a time, at first moving slowly, then becoming almost maniacal with one snap of the shutter after the other.

He was so engrossed in what he was doing, he jumped when he heard the feminine voice behind him. "Mr. Holloway, what are you doing here?"

Nathan spun around and found himself face-to-face with one of the teachers from the elementary school. Stephanie Mansfield. A slow grin covered his face, and he felt a surge of energy flow through him. She must have followed him. That brought him more pleasure than he ever imagined it would.

"Same thing you're doing here," he replied. "Watching the sunset." No need to embarrass her for chasing after him.

She folded her arms across her chest and looked downright smug. "I didn't come here to watch the sunset," she said softly.

So, she was going to come right out and admit her crush on him? What a pleasant surprise. Maybe this trip to Hartsville wouldn't be so bad after all.

"I live here," she added, then clamped her jaw shut with a determination he hadn't seen on any woman. Ever.

He was stunned. "You live here?"

She nodded. "Yes."

"Where?" he asked, holding his arms out and glancing around.

"That house over there," she answered, pointing to

the cottage he'd peered into when he first arrived. "It was my grandmother's, and she left it to me."

Nathan's shock was so great, he was speechless. All he could do was just stand there with his mouth hanging open.

"By yourself?"

"I've lived here by myself for three years, and I like it," she said. "It suits me."

He had to swallow in order to talk. "This is a long way out for a single woman."

Shaking her head and rolling her eyes, she replied, "I do just fine. In fact, I can do anything anyone else can do."

"Yes," he said, finally coming to his senses. "I can see that." Why had he acted like such a sexist jerk?

"Why did you come here?" she asked.

"I just wanted a pretty spot to watch the sunset, and I wound up here. I hope you don't mind."

Stephanie smiled. She was downright gorgeous when she allowed her full mouth to widen in a smile. The urge to whip out his camera and start snapping pictures of her was almost too great to resist. But he refrained. He had the feeling she wouldn't appreciate him doing that. At least, not now.

"No, I don't mind. I'm just flattered that you like my place enough to take pictures of it." Then her face took on a look of panic. "But I hope you don't plan to put it in a magazine. I don't want people traipsing all over my property just because you decided to make it famous."

He had to laugh. It was too hard not to, she was so serious. "Don't worry, Miss Mansfield. I won't put these pictures in any magazines. They're for me."

Relief washed over her face. "That's good." She backed away from him, leaving him wanting more. "Let me know if you need anything." Then she turned her back and walked toward her house.

"Miss Mansfield," he called out before she could get too far away from him. "Are you going to Ed's, er, I mean Mr. Phillips's house tonight?"

She turned around and looked at him strangely. "Why would I go to Mr. Phillips's house?"

He shrugged. "I don't know. I was just wondering."

"N-no, I'm not going to his house tonight," she stuttered. It was cute, watching her wonder what in the world he was talking about. "I don't know why you'd ask me that."

"Never mind," he said as he forced himself to turn back around and look at the sun that was in prime position for another snapshot.

Once Nathan was alone again, he tried hard to get back into the mood he'd been in earlier, but it was impossible. Without Stephanie Mansfield beside him, he felt strangely empty. It was nice having her there.

She's in the house, he told himself. *All you have*

to do is walk right up to the door and knock. But he couldn't. At least not now.

But why not? Who said he couldn't go to her door and ask her to join him tonight when he went to Ed Phillips's house? Surely Ed wouldn't mind.

As soon as Nathan got all the pictures he could take before he needed to leave, he gathered up his things and headed for his car. Now that he knew who lived there, he looked at it from a different perspective. It really was adorable. Well kept, freshly painted. And there was a single row of flowers across the front. Not too many. Just enough to add color and make it inviting.

That's what the house was—inviting. Knowing that Stephanie Mansfield lived there made him wish she'd follow through with what the flowers started. He wanted to go inside and see how she lived, to inhale the aroma that certainly must have filled the kitchen. She looked like someone who would bake gingerbread. A warmth flooded him at the mere thought of that.

As soon as he piled all his things in the car, Nathan went to the house and knocked. Stephanie was there in a matter of seconds.

"Yes?" She held the door open enough so he could see her full length, clad in leggings and a thin sweater—quite different from the dress she wore to school.

"I was, uh, wondering," he began as his gaze raked her from head to toe. Man, was she comfortable on the eyes.

"You were wondering?" There she went again with that wide smile.

Nathan took a deep breath and plunged in. "I'd like for you to accompany me to Ed Phillips's house this evening."

Her smile faded to a frown. "I'm not sure that would be acceptable."

"Not acceptable?" he asked. *What was wrong with that?*

"No," she said, shaking her head. "He's my boss, and he didn't invite me. Maybe you'd better go alone."

Nathan reached in his back pocket and pulled out his cell phone. "Let me make a quick call."

She mysteriously vanished, he suspected, to give him privacy. He dialed Ed's number from memory and told him what he wanted.

Ed sounded surprised. "You're at her house? How in the world did you ever find her place? It's way out in the sticks."

Nathan felt defensive. "Actually, it's quite nice." He stuck his head in the door and took a quick glance around. "I love what she did with all the wood and brass."

"Well, if you want to invite her, I suppose that's fine. It's just that . . ."

"Just that what, Ed?" Nathan asked. "Were you planning to introduce me to someone, or something? You know how I feel about matchmaking."

"Oh, no, I wouldn't do anything like that," Ed quickly replied. Too quickly, in fact. "Not after what happened in college."

Nathan chuckled at the memory. "That was a long time ago."

"Yes, it's fine if you bring Miss Mansfield, if that's what you want. Just don't get too wrapped up in one person while you're in town, Nathan. There are scores of people who want to meet you."

Nathan clicked the phone off and let himself into the house. "Stephanie?" No answer. "Stephanie?" he called a little bit louder. Still no answer. "Miss Mansfield?"

Suddenly she appeared at the doorway leading to the hall. "Did you need me for something?"

"Yes," he said. "I really want you to go with me to Ed's house tonight."

Her eyes widened in amazement. "Are you sure it's okay?"

Nodding, Nathan said, "I just called him, and he said he'd love to have you over."

"Well," she said as she wiped her hands on the front of her sweater. "I guess I can go. But I can't stay out too late. I have lesson plans to work on."

Lesson plans. Now that was a first. Nathan thought he'd heard it all until this. But then again he'd never gone out with a schoolteacher before. He'd been seen around the city mostly with models. Egotistical models. Models who were more worried about their skin staying hydrated than having a good time.

"Let me change clothes and grab a jacket. It's supposed to get cool tonight."

Nathan didn't think he'd notice if the thermometer dropped twenty degrees. Whenever he was around Stephanie he felt warm all over. And that was something that never happened to him.

It took her less than ten minutes to change clothes and put her hair up. Another first.

"Are you sure you don't want me to take my car?" she asked. "It's a long way. I'd hate for you to have to drive all the way out here just to take me home and then turn right around and go back to your hotel."

"Trust me, Stephanie," he said. "I don't mind." He opened her door, helped her in, and ran around to the driver's side. As he got into the car, he turned to her and asked, "Do you mind if I call you Stephanie? It seems strange to call you Miss Mansfield."

"No, I don't mind. Just don't do it in front of the children. They know me as Miss Mansfield, and I don't want them to form any bad habits. You know how children are."

No, he didn't know how children were, but he was willing to learn. That is, if Stephanie was willing to teach him.

All the way into town, he asked questions about her house and how she came to live all the way out in the country, all by herself. He already knew her grandmother had left it to her, but he wanted to know the details about why she hadn't chosen to sell it and get something closer to the school.

She shrugged. "I love it out there. It brings back wonderful memories."

"Did you go there a lot when you were a kid?"

"My parents died in a car crash when I was still a toddler, so my grandmother raised me."

"I'm sorry," he said. Why did he have to ask so many questions? He'd better shut up or he'd wind up in territory he couldn't handle.

Then she turned to him. "And how about you? How did you get into photography?"

He let out a sigh of relief. Nathan could handle this, now that they were on familiar turf. "Someone gave me an instant camera when I was in third grade, and I literally wore the thing out."

"An instant camera?"

Nathan nodded. "It didn't take good pictures, but at least I was able to capture moments to make them last. When that camera finally died, I used my small savings and went out and purchased my first decent camera. It still wasn't the best, but it sure did take good pictures. Or so I thought at the time."

"And that's what got you to where you are now?" she asked.

"Well, not exactly," he replied. "I kept learning photography, and my parents let me put a darkroom in the basement when they saw how much I was spending to have my pictures developed at the local drugstore. In high school, I got on the newspaper and yearbook staffs and took pictures of everything that crossed my path."

Stephanie laughed. It was a sincere laugh, complete with full smile and crinkling eyes. That was another thing he wasn't used to. Most of the models he knew didn't want wrinkles, so they didn't smile with their whole faces.

"I can just see you running all over the place with your camera. Did you ever see yourself doing what you do now?"

Nathan shook his head. "Never in a million years. In fact, I was such a goof-off in school, I think the teachers gave me passing grades just to get rid of me."

He thought she was beautiful when she smiled, but it didn't hold a candle to when she laughed. Her eyes lit up like sunshine, and her face took on a rosy glow that warmed him from the inside out. No other woman had affected him like that.

"You think I'm kidding?"

"Somehow, I don't see you being a goof-off, Nathan. You're so focused."

He cast a quick glance at her, then turned back to

the road. "Only when I'm taking pictures. Nothing else interests me much."

"You seem to enjoy being around Mr. Phillips," she said. Her body was turned toward him, and he got a glimpse of the whole effect of her entire being.

Stephanie Mansfield was different. She carried herself differently than the other women he saw in Hartsville. She had a certain poise that alluded to a self-confidence that her words belied.

Nathan nodded. "Yes, Ed and I go way back. We were roommates in college."

"That's what you said earlier. How did the two of you get together in the first place?"

"Neither of us knew anyone on campus, so we left our fate to the dormitory computers."

"You did?" she asked in wide-eyed wonder. "I'm surprised you stuck it out. Most of the time those computers spit out disasters."

"I know," he replied as he inhaled deeply to catch the drift of her fragrance. What was it? It was vaguely familiar, but he couldn't figure out what it was. Maybe he'd ask later, when he was more comfortable in doing so. "We got lucky."

"You seem so different," she said softly.

"We're as different as night and day," he agreed. "That's probably what kept us friends."

"Yeah, I've heard that opposites often attract," she said.

Was that what he and Stephanie were? Opposites? He sure was attracted to her.

Nathan glanced at his watch, "I can't believe this."

"What?"

"We're early."

Stephanie glanced from right to left, then back at Nathan. "Then let's go for a short drive."

"Any ideas where you'd like to go?"

She shrugged. "I can show you the sights of Hartsville in about ten minutes."

"Then let's do it."

Stephanie pointed to the statue propped in the middle of the town square and told him the history of how a Civil War battle was fought there. Then she directed him to the teen hangout, the Dairy Swirl. "I used to spend every single Saturday night right there in that front booth," she said, pointing to the well-lit café.

How adorable. Nathan could picture her sitting there with a table full of friends, all drinking milk shakes and ogling the guys as they drove by in their old cars.

"Of course, most of the girls I went with left with guys, but I generally went home alone," she said with a note of sadness in her voice.

Nathan was surprised. But then of course Ed Phillips hadn't recognized Stephanie's beauty, so why should he expect anyone else from this place to? Their standards must be different, he figured.

After seeing the feed store and the original gas station with round pump heads, Stephanie made the announcement that he'd seen everything that really mattered in Hartsville.

"Oh, I went to the Do Drop Inn Diner for lunch with Ed today," Nathan said proudly. He kept the part about the indigestion to himself for fear that she might be offended.

But she wasn't offended. Instead, she crinkled her nose. "Did you like it?"

"Well," he began, trying hard to come up with something neutral. "It's not the kind of place you'll find in New York."

"Good for New York. Those people have good taste not to let the Do Drop Inn set up shop there." Her expression was adorable, and Nathan let out a chuckle he'd been trying hard to hold back.

"You don't like it?" he asked.

"No. The Dairy Swirl is much better. They have soft-serve ice cream."

Nathan reached over and patted her hand. He tried to stop himself. Touching her was dangerous for him, with the attraction he already felt. But he couldn't resist. "We'll have to have ice cream there before I return to New York."

Chapter Three

Stephanie swiftly pulled her hand into her lap and stared straight ahead. "We're almost there."

Nathan couldn't for the life of him figure out what had caused her to react as she had. Perhaps she'd been hurt in the past. Or maybe she just wasn't interested. He knew he'd be better off leaving the whole thing alone, but he wanted to know more about her. He intended to find out.

There were already several people at Ed's house when they walked inside. Nathan shook the men's hands and smiled at the ladies who didn't act like they wanted to shake hands.

Miss Pritchett was there, all decked out in pink, her frizzy blond hair pouffed out with little butterfly clips in the sides. And she smelled strongly of department store perfume, unlike the subtle fragrance he detected when he was with Stephanie.

"Hi, there, Nathan," Miss Pritchett said, batting her false eyelashes at him. *No subtlety there, that's for sure.*

"Hello, Miss Pritchett," he replied.

"Oh, call me Pamela," she cooed.

"Pamela," he said, nodding. Then he turned to Stephanie who'd stood there watching, taking it all in. "Want a drink?"

She shrugged.

Nathan placed his hand in the small of her back and gently guided her toward the kitchen. "What would you like?"

"To go home," she stated flatly.

Nathan was taken aback by that comment. He turned on his heel and found himself looking into the eyes of a teary-eyed woman. "What? We just got here."

"I know," she said. "But I need to go home. I don't belong here."

Somehow, without her having to say a word, Nathan knew. He knew that Stephanie had never been part of this group, and she was uncomfortable. Their loss.

"Look, Stephanie, you're with me. You belong here just as much as I do." He desperately wanted to make her feel wanted. He really liked her. How could he tell her without her thinking he was just trying to be nice?

She closed her eyes, inhaled deeply, and slowly let it out. He saw the pain etched on her face. More than anything he wanted to do whatever it took to make it go away.

Without thinking, Nathan reached out and pulled her to his chest. She resisted at first, but in a matter of seconds, she relaxed and leaned into him. He felt a slight shudder as she let out a stifled sob.

Her back was to the rest of the kitchen, so only he could see her face as he tilted it up toward his. "Stephanie, I wanted you here with me because I find you the most attractive and appealing woman in town."

"You do?" she asked incredulously.

"Yes, I do." He leaned to the side and looked around. "In fact, you're more beautiful than most of the models I photograph. But that's not why I'm here with you."

Her lips quivered as she eased into a grin. "Tell me why." Her gaze dropped, then she looked back at him from beneath her naturally long eyelashes. "Please," she whispered.

"Because you've got class." He meant it, too. "And you don't seem to be caught up in the silliness the rest of them are caught up in. It's like they never left high school."

Stephanie tilted her head up, her chin still quivering slightly. But he saw the pride. The pride that probably got her through some difficult times here in Hartsville.

What he wanted to know was why she'd returned to the place where she didn't feel like she fit in. The other women obviously had hurt her, and the men virtually ignored her to the point of making her feel unworthy of being here. But there was something about her that spoke of self-confidence, especially in the school. She wasn't totally without self-esteem.

The other women all had signs of hard living and plastic surgery, and their hair had been permed and dyed to the point of making it frizzy. Stephanie was all natural.

As soon as she looked like she'd recovered, Nathan extended his arm. "Shall we join the party now, Stephanie?"

With a big heart-warming grin and a twinkle replacing the teary mist in her eye, she tucked her hand in the crook of his elbow and said, "Sure. I'd love that."

Together, the two of them walked back into the living room where a small group had gathered around the stereo. Ed had a stack of CDs that he was looking through, and a couple of the women were dancing in place. Stephanie tightened her grip on his arm.

When Ed saw that his old college roommate had

joined the party, he bellowed, "Looks like the guest of honor is here. What would you like to listen to?"

Nathan tilted his head and scratched his chin. "Do you have 'You Are the Sunshine of My Life'?"

Ed's head snapped up, and his jaw dropped. Nathan saw how his old friend stared first at him, then at Stephanie, like he couldn't figure out what was going on between the two of them.

Stephanie saw that Mr. Phillips was still shocked at the fact that Nathan wanted to be with her rather than one of the other women he probably considered more suitable for a hotshot, big-city photographer. Even she wasn't clear why. But it sure did feel good for a change.

When he looked down at her, she felt all tingly. In fact, she now knew what it was like to be the object of her crush's attention.

"Uh, sure, Nathan," Mr. Phillips said in response to Nathan's music request. "I'm sure it's in here somewhere."

It was actually quite comical watching her boss flit from one side of his entertainment center to the other looking all over the place for a song that had long been outdated. The expressions of the other women in the room were priceless, too. It was like they couldn't believe what they were seeing.

Nathan leaned over and whispered something in her ear, and she giggled. He'd told her that anyone in New York would have made an excuse not to play something so old, then put on whatever they wanted to. But this was Hartsville, the place where people bent over backward to make you feel at home in their living rooms.

Finally, Ed found what he was looking for. "Here it is, Nathan." Then, with pride, he put the CD in the player.

Without missing a beat, Nathan turned her toward him, gently wrapped both arms around her waist, and pulled her toward him in a fluid motion. She didn't even have to think what to do next. It was like her arms had minds of their own, moving up his chest and resting on his shoulders. They swayed in time to the music, leaving everyone in the room standing there, their mouths agape. She closed her eyes and enjoyed the moment.

Stephanie felt like she was in a dream world. This couldn't be happening to her, she thought. It wasn't real. Soon the alarm clock would go off, and she'd have to get up to teach school.

But when the music stopped and she opened her eyes, she was still in Nathan's arms. And he was looking at her with open admiration. Her heart pounded so hard she was afraid it would jump out of her mouth.

"Stephanie," he whispered. "Thank you for the dance."

She opened her mouth, but nothing would come

out but a squeak. Quickly she closed it and smiled back at him. Everyone else had long since scattered, and they were trying their best not to gawk. But Stephanie knew they were all watching. She'd lived in Hartsville long enough to know that they were as shocked as she was. After all, she was only Stephanie Mansfield, not Pamela Pritchett, homecoming queen, sweetheart of the Hartsville football team. Stephanie's greatest claim to fame was the fact that she'd decorated the prize-winning float that year.

The evening went by like a dream. A very cloudy dream. But soon it was time to leave. Most of the people present were teachers and school administrators who had to go to work the next day.

"It's been fun, Ed," Nathan said as he pumped his friend's hand. "And thanks for introducing me to Stephanie."

Mr. Phillips glanced nervously toward Stephanie, and she felt a smile threatening to grab hold of her lips. But she resisted. She raised her eyebrows and said a sincere, "Thank you very much for a wonderful party."

Then they left. Nathan held the door for her as she got into his rental car.

As soon as he pulled out of the driveway, Nathan let his head fall back and he belted out a good laugh.

"What's so funny?" Stephanie asked.

"I think that's the first time I've seen Ed speechless."

Stephanie saw it, too. Although she suspected Nathan didn't have a clue why, she knew the reason Mr. Phillips acted so funny. Nathan could have had his pick of many teachers at the school, but for some unknown reason, he chose to take her to the party. And she hadn't even been invited.

Nathan turned to her and patted her hand, his expression one of kindness and compassion. "Don't let them get to you, Stephanie. You outclass every last one of them, including Ed."

"But I thought Ed was your friend," Stephanie said with a lump in her throat. Nathan was aware of more than he was saying. She could tell by the way he spoke to her.

"He is. But that still doesn't excuse his behavior."

With a shrug, Stephanie said, "He's always been very nice to me. I can't complain." Sure, Mr. Phillips had been nice, but he'd never included her in any of the social life she was fully aware of. He was a few years older than her and several of the other teachers who'd returned to their hometown, but once they became adults, the clique seemed to encompass all age groups.

"What's the big deal with Miss Pritchett?" he asked.

Stephanie turned to look at him, and he winked at her, a smile on his lips. "Pamela Pritchett has always been the Hartsville sweetheart, ever since she was a little girl. When we had the rodeo pageant, she was the princess. And no one ever dared to run against her for anything she was in because it would have been futile."

"Maybe that's the problem," Nathan said. "No one ever ran against her. I would have voted for you."

Stephanie smiled, in spite of the fact that Nathan was saying silly things. She couldn't help it. And she had to admit, it felt nice to have a man say this.

"I've got a couple more days to take pictures of the teachers, then Ed asked me to work on restoring some old pictures of the school when it was first built. That should keep me in town through the weekend. I have a few shots to take of some teachers early next week, too."

"Sounds like this is quite a project," Stephanie responded. "I'm looking forward to seeing the finished product."

Nodding, Nathan said, "Everything Ed does is first rate. I have to give him credit for that."

Stephanie settled back in the seat as they drove out to her house. She enjoyed the silence, but she wasn't so sure Nathan appreciated it. Most people she knew loved constant chatter, but not her. There were so many other sounds that were missed when people talked nonstop.

Nathan almost missed the turnoff, but Stephanie pointed to it before he drove past it. He pulled in front of her house and helped her out of the car.

As he walked her to the front door, Stephanie

pulled her keys from her purse. She turned to him and stuck out her hand. "I had a lovely time, Nathan. Thank you for inviting me."

He took her hand and held it for several seconds as their gazes locked. Stephanie felt her blood begin to heat up and the tingle all the way to her toes. She never wanted the moment to end.

But Nathan finally let go of her hand. "If we were in New York, I'd ask to come in. But this isn't New York, and you have to be at the school early in the morning, so I'll just say good-bye for now."

"Good night, Nathan," Stephanie whispered.

Nathan reached out and pulled Stephanie toward him. She was thrown temporarily off-balance, but he steadied her against his chest. As he tilted her chin up to face him, Stephanie didn't know what to do. This had never happened to her before.

Sure, she'd kissed a few guys back in college, but no one had ever made her feel so special. She inhaled deeply and held it. He grinned. "I don't want you to hyperventilate, Stephanie. Just relax."

She let the air out of her lungs in a ragged breath, and he leaned over and planted a soft, gentle kiss on her lips. Then he backed away.

"See you in the morning, Stephanie."

He waited for her to unlock her door and go inside before he turned and left. As she listened to the sound of his car driving away, she leaned against the door and sighed. This was one night she needed to deposit in her memory bank. She never wanted to forget the magic of the evening.

Lying in bed a few minutes later, Stephanie luxuriated in the memories of what she'd shared with Nathan. The strong, steady rhythm of his heart beating against hers as they danced would forever be up there with her favorite moments. He held her tight and made her feel as though she were the most special and beautiful woman in the world, in spite of all the gawks and stares from the rest of the people from her hometown.

Mr. Phillips didn't even try to hide his surprise at Nathan's choice of companion for the evening. It had been obvious that he'd invited Pamela as well as a few backup women for the famous photographer to choose from.

But Nathan had chosen her to spend the evening with. And she did feel special.

Stephanie hugged her pillow close and fell asleep with wonderful thoughts and feelings. Morning came much too quickly.

Nathan rubbed his eyes and took a long look around the room. Where was he?

He sat up and then he remembered. He was in Hartsville on a project for his old college chum. Time to go to work.

As Nathan let the sleepiness wash away in the shower, he remembered the sweetness of Stephanie

Mansfield. She reminded him of a character in some old movie, where the beautiful star didn't see her own beauty, which made her all the more attractive to him. And she was positively the most incredible person he'd ever met. She not only loved being a teacher, she loved children, and she took each and every one of their interests to heart. He had no doubt that she'd lay her life on the line for her students.

"That woman would make a great mother," he mumbled to himself as he toweled off.

Nathan had a feeling that Ed didn't ignore Stephanie on purpose. He suspected it was something that had begun long ago, way back when all these people were children. They had a social order, and the boundaries were solid, making it extremely difficult for anyone to ever cross over, regardless of how they wound up as adults.

That was one of the things he loved about New York. People didn't seem to care where you came from, and they certainly didn't consider a small-town homecoming queen anything special.

He had to admit, though, that there were some appealing qualities of Hartsville. First of all, people actually stopped you on the street and asked how you were doing. And the school was safe from anyone the administrators didn't know, because everyone knew everyone else.

Overall, this was probably a very nice place to raise children, but he still had a hard time with the social caste. It seemed to be accepted by everyone here, but it appeared awfully snobby to Nathan.

I guess there are just some things I'll never understand.

The school was close to his hotel, but he still chose to drive. No telling what the weather would be like later on, when it was time to leave.

Ed was standing outside, greeting children as they piled off the school bus, when Nathan pulled up in the visitors' parking lot. That was one of the things Nathan had always liked about Ed. He was a wonderful greeter. And in college, if it weren't for Ed, Nathan wouldn't have known anyone up close and personal. He would have remained hidden behind his camera.

As soon as Ed spotted Nathan, he motioned for him to come over. "I'm glad you could make it last night, but I'm worried about something, Nathan."

"What's that?" Nathan had never known Ed to worry about anything. He'd always taken problems and fixed them before he had time to waste energy worrying.

"You don't seem to be having a good time here in Hartsville." Ed waved to another busload of children as they jumped down from the high steps, then turned to face Nathan.

"I'm having fun," Nathan argued.

With a soft chuckle, Ed shook his head. "You don't have to take on Miss Mansfield, Nathan. There are plenty of women who are dying to get to know you. Look around. This town may be small, but it's not hurting for good-looking women."

"No, that's true," Nathan agreed. How could he say this without upsetting his friend? He couldn't think of any way but to just be blunt. "But I happen to find Miss Mansfield very attractive."

"You're kidding," Ed said, genuinely flabbergasted. "She's always been the sweet, brainy type."

"And I find that attractive."

"But why would you want her when Pamela Pritchett is so eager to get to know you better?" Ed had stopped pretending to pay attention, and he'd turned to face Nathan directly.

Nathan shook his head and chewed on the inside of his lip for a moment before answering. "I just happen to think that Stephanie Mansfield is the most attractive woman I've met in a long time."

"That's amazing," Ed finally said after he had a moment to recover. "You're the only person who has ever said that."

"Maybe so, but I think everyone around here must be blind not to see it." Nathan turned toward the front door of the school and started walking away. "Now if you don't mind, I need to get inside. I've got work to do."

"By all means," Ed said, nodding, "go ahead. Don't let me keep you from our masterpiece."

Nathan never should have taken this job. He

should have known that it was a ploy for Ed to show off a little to his hometown cronies, to be able to say he was tight friends with a famous photographer. It was now obvious to Nathan, but it was too late to stop the project. He'd already committed.

Stephanie stood at her classroom window and watched Nathan as he parted ways with Mr. Phillips. She could tell that they weren't talking about academic things, based on their body language. And she had a feeling that her boss had mentioned something about last night.

She stepped back and closed her eyes, sighing. *Last night. Oh, what a night!*

Never in her life had Stephanie had such a dreamy experience. She had to pinch herself several times to know for sure it was real and not a figment of her imagination.

Stephanie was used to the people from her hometown saying things that had once hurt her, and the pain wasn't so sharp anymore. In fact, it was almost comforting to know that some things just never changed.

But when Nathan Holloway came to town, he didn't come with any preconceived notions about the people of Hartsville, and he'd chosen her. He had virtually ignored all the other women, the beauty queens who were used to all the attention and adulation, choosing instead to be with her. How had she gotten so lucky?

The first bell of the day hadn't rung yet, so most of the children were still outside on the playground waiting for school to start. Mostly she heard the voices of teachers as they filed from the teachers' lounge to their classrooms, and they had to walk right by her classroom.

The voices of Pamela Pritchett and Marla Sawyer drew closer, and Stephanie strained to hear what they were talking about. She stepped closer to the door to better hear them. Marla had never cared for Pamela, so there was no telling what was being said between them.

"I think it's sweet for Nathan to be paying so much attention to Stephanie," Pamela said in her condescending tone. "She's always been such a pitiful wallflower. Maybe this is what she needs to come out of her shell."

Stephanie felt her blood run cold, and she almost plugged her ears with her fingers. That was the last thing she needed to hear.

Marla belted out a hearty laugh. "Steph's no wallflower. In fact, you might want to take a good look at her. If she's any kind of flower, she's one who's in full bloom."

Good for Marla. It was a noble attempt to stick up for the underdog, but Stephanie knew it was futile.

No one ever went up against Pamela Pritchett and won. In her own sweet-faced way, Pamela got whatever her little heart desired.

"Eddie was shocked, but he promised it was all just Nathan's kind heart that made him do such a ridiculous thing. In fact, Eddie's hosting another party, a much more intimate deal. He's inviting a few couples, and he's telling Nathan that he can't bring anyone else."

"You don't say," Marla said, stopping in front of her classroom. "Does Nathan know what *Eddie's* up to?"

The sound of Pamela's laughter filled Stephanie's classroom. "Oh, I'm sure he's well aware of me by now. In fact, when he was dancing with Stephanie, I couldn't help but notice how he kept looking around, scanning the crowd, probably hoping I'd rescue him from his mission."

Stephanie waited a few seconds for Pamela to leave, then she went to the door of her classroom. Marla was still standing there, staring down the hall.

She jerked her head up when Stephanie appeared before her. "You heard that, didn't you?"

Stephanie nodded.

"Don't pay a bit of attention to it. It's her ego and genuine snobbery talking."

With a deep sigh, Stephanie shook her head. "No, I'm not stupid, Marla. I know she's probably right. But at least I had a good time last night."

Marla tossed her hair over her shoulder in disgust and complete loyalty to Stephanie. "Well, I, for one, don't believe Nathan Holloway would have to go to such extremes to make someone feel good. A big smile from that gorgeous face and a simple touch would be all he'd need to do. I have a feeling he doesn't see things from a small-town perspective."

"I wish you were right, Marla," Stephanie said, now fully resigned to agreeing with Pamela, as much as she didn't want to. "But I'm also realistic. I know who I am, and I'm no Pamela Pritchett."

"That's for sure," Marla agreed. "Thank goodness."

Then the bell rang. Time to get to work.

The morning went by so fast Stephanie didn't have a chance to think about what she'd overheard earlier. Then she decided to grab something from the cafeteria and have lunch in her room so she could finish her lesson plans for the week. Last night she had been too tired to work on it when she got in.

Somehow she managed to get a tray of food all the way to her desk without being noticed. Normally, she ate with Marla and a few other teachers in the lounge.

She'd just picked up a buttered roll when she felt the presence of someone else in the room. It was Nathan, standing at the door, leaning against the frame, his arms folded, a smile on his lips. Wow, was he good to look at.

Stephanie quickly dropped her bread and smiled back. "Can I do something for you, Mr. Holloway?"

His smile instantly turned to a frown. "What's with the Mr. Holloway business? I'm Nathan, remember?"

"Sorry, Nathan," Stephanie said, casting her glance downward. She had a hard time facing him after what she'd overheard Pamela saying that morning.

"I'd kind of hoped we could have lunch together," he said, not budging from his position by the door.

"Well, I do have a lot of work to do that I should have done last night," she said, still not daring to look him in the eye.

"Oh, I'm sorry," he said, his voice genuinely apologetic. "I'll leave you alone then."

Stephanie waited until she knew he was gone before dropping her face into her hands and letting a single tear fall. She would have loved to have had lunch with Nathan, but she didn't dare risk putting her heart in any more jeopardy than it was already in. She could definitely imagine herself falling hard and fast for this man.

Had he said something wrong? Had he offended her? Or was that the royal brush-off Stephanie Mansfield had just given him?

It had happened before, and Nathan was certain it would happen again, but she seemed to be having fun last night. What could have changed between then and now? Had Ed told her about some of his shenanigans back in college? Probably. But even so, he couldn't imagine someone holding that against him now.

Something else must have come up. Maybe she had someone else in her life. He did an about-face and headed toward Ed's office behind the reception desk at the front of the school.

After a brief knock at the door, Ed said, "Come in, Nathan."

Nathan walked right in and said, "What's up with Stephanie Mansfield? Do you have any idea why she's avoiding me?"

Ed shrugged, but Nathan didn't miss the smug look of relief on his face. "Who knows why women do anything?"

Without having to be asked, Nathan sat down in one of the upholstered leather chairs in the office. "I'd hoped to have lunch with her, but she ran like a little mouse with her tray, all the way to her classroom."

"She's never been the social type," Ed advised. "Maybe you'd better stick with people who are more like you."

Nathan knew better than to argue. From what he'd seen, Ed would never understand; he was so caught up in the inner workings of this small town. While Hartsville was charming, it was frustrating, too. People didn't allow others to live down reputations, no matter what they did.

"So, what can I do for you, Nathan?" Ed asked as he leaned back and crossed his ankle over his knee.

With a deep sigh, Nathan replied, "I guess there isn't anything you can do. I'll just have to get over it."

"Then you'll want to hear what I have planned for this weekend," Ed said, his eyes sparkling with delight.

"What's that?"

"A very small, intimate dinner at my house with a few people I'd like for you to get to know."

"Oh, no you don't," Nathan said as he stood up from his chair. "I'm not interested in getting fixed up with someone you pick for me."

"Come on, Nathan. Stephanie's obviously not in-terested in you, and you're in town. You don't have anything else to do Saturday night, do you?"

"Well . . ." Nathan's voice trailed off as he thought about it. He didn't have a thing to do. He'd been hoping Stephanie might want to go for a drive and maybe even stop at the Dairy Swirl, but she'd just brushed him off. "Okay, I'll be there."

"Good. How's six o'clock?"

In New York, no one would have started their din-ner party at 6:00, but this wasn't New York. It was Hartsville, where the sidewalks rolled up at sunset. "Six o'clock sounds just fine."

As Nathan left the principal's office, he heard Ed pick up the phone and dial. He hesitated for a moment to hear who he'd called. That was when he heard, "Miss Pritchett, could you come to the office immediately, please?"

Ed didn't waste any time paging Pamela Pritchett over the intercom, Nathan thought as he resumed walking out the door. Oh well, at least he'd have someone who wanted to talk to him. Too bad it wasn't who he wanted to be with, though. *I guess you can't have everything.*

Nathan was almost to the door of his makeshift studio when Pamela Pritchett came barreling around the corner, adjusting the skirt that was just a little too tight for a kindergarten teacher. She would have collided with him if he hadn't seen her. He just took a step out of her way.

Chapter Four

"Oh," she exclaimed with breathlessness. "Sorry, Nathan, I didn't see you."

"That's quite all right, Miss Pritchett," he replied.

"Please call me Pamela," she cooed.

"If you don't mind, I'd rather call you Miss Pritchett." He noticed the look of disappointment on her face. "At least here at school. The students might be listening."

"Oh, yeah," she said, her voice now husky. "You're right."

"See ya, Miss Pritchett." He offered her a mock salute, and her face reddened, a contrived blush, he was certain.

"Okay, Mr. Holloway," she said in response just a little too loudly to be natural, then winked.

He cringed.

That afternoon, Nathan took pictures of the few male teachers at the school. Since they wore more subdued colors, he had a different backdrop for them and the lighting had to be adjusted as well. After being surrounded by females all day, having male subjects was nice for a change of pace.

Nathan was just finishing up with the last teacher, and he was about to put his equipment away when Marla showed up at the door. "May I come in?" she asked.

For some reason, Nathan didn't get the same feeling from Marla Sawyer that he got from most of the other teachers. Maybe because she was married; he didn't know. But whatever the case, he knew he could relax around her.

"What can I do for you?" he asked as he began to pack his camera in the case.

"It's about Stephanie."

He glanced up from his camera and looked directly at her. "What about Stephanie?"

"I don't want her to get hurt," she said, not averting her gaze a single bit. He could tell she meant business, but he wasn't quite certain what business she was into.

"Don't worry," he said after a long pause. "I have no intention of hurting her."

"Good," she said as she began to back toward the door.

"Is that all you wanted?"

"That's it."

Nathan was puzzled. People around here didn't talk in complete thoughts. They said cryptic messages and left the rest up to the listener to figure out.

One thing he did know was that Marla sincerely liked Stephanie. She was doing her best to be a good friend, but he still didn't understand what was going on. Oh well, who was he to try to figure it out? Just an outsider who didn't have a clue.

As he finished packing his equipment, Nathan tried his best to keep his mind void of all Hartsville business. No sense in making something big out of the actions of these people. He was here for two reasons: to do an old friend a favor and to take a break from his normal daily activities. And he'd be glad to get back to his studio in New York where people *always* said what they meant and *sometimes* meant what they said. Maybe New York was crazy, too, he considered. But at least he was used to that kind of craziness.

"I don't think you have a thing to worry about," Marla said as she walked with Stephanie to the faculty parking lot.

"Who's worried?" Stephanie said as she walked straight and kept her eyes focused on where she was going. She didn't want to alarm her friend, but she felt sick about Nathan going to the dinner party with Pamela.

"You are, and you know it," Marla said. "Look at you. You can't even concentrate long enough to wear your sweater right side out."

Stephanie quickly glanced down and fidgeted with her sweater. "I was cold, and I didn't have time to fix it."

"Sure you didn't."

"Come on, Marla. Quit badgering me about Nathan Holloway. He's not interested in me. He's just a very nice man who wants to make me feel special."

"I don't think so, Steph," Marla said as they stopped by Stephanie's car. "I think he's really interested in you, but everyone's making it hard for him to follow through with his intentions."

"You've always been romantic, Marla," Stephanie said, forcing a laugh. "You should have gone into acting."

"Don't say I didn't tell you," Marla said in response as she moved away and headed for her own car. "You'll be hearing from him again. Mark my word."

" 'Bye," Stephanie called over her shoulder, then she turned to her car and unlocked it. "Dreamer," she whispered to herself.

As soon as she got the engine started, Stephanie turned on the radio and pushed the button of the local talk radio station. The famous nationally syndicated psychologist was on the air, and she was talking to someone about family relationships. Stephanie punched another button. The last thing she needed to listen to was a discussion of relationships.

If only her grandmother hadn't left her house to her, she would have had no excuse to return to Hartsville. Sure, she loved the place because it was where she'd grown up. There was comfort in being in familiar surroundings.

But there was also pain.

Pain from having everyone in town remembering the awkward stages, of pigtails being cut off and tossed around the playground. Pain from being the only girl in high school who wore both braces and glasses. "Metal Mouth" and "Four Eyes" were names she knew she'd never live down.

Ed Phillips had been the star quarterback on the high school football team when she was only a freshman. He knew who she was, only because she tutored some of the members of the junior varsity team, and he was often with them when they met. He knew her as "the Brain."

Pamela was in the same class as Stephanie, but they'd been in a different league socially. While Stephanie's friends weren't the nerds and geeks, she wasn't one of the most popular girls during her teenage years. Pamela was.

When Ed Phillips came to town from college,

everyone knew about it. Parties were thrown in his honor, and people stopped on the street to talk about it.

He'd majored in physical education, and he'd gone on to coach a high school football team in another town while he worked on his master's degree in school administration. The Hartsville school board wanted him back so badly, they offered him the principal's position as soon as it became available. And naturally, he'd taken it.

All Stephanie ever heard about when she came home from college was how wonderful Ed Phillips was. And she'd heard that Pamela Pritchett had changed her major from fashion merchandising to elementary education so she could have summers off to travel.

Somehow, Stephanie couldn't imagine Pamela teaching little kids, but because she was such good friends with Ed and his buddies, she snagged the job Stephanie had wanted from the beginning. Stephanie was offered the only vacant position at the school—teaching fourth-graders.

At first, she'd been disappointed, because she thought she'd have behavior problems. But once she got started and learned the ropes, understanding the development issues of nine-year-olds, Stephanie was thankful to have children at such an exciting stage of their lives.

Teaching in Hartsville had been a mixed blessing.

On one hand, she was happy to be in a familiar place where she didn't have to learn her way around. She'd gone to this same school as a small child, and most of her memories were good, as long as she thought of the academic things. On the other hand, though, she couldn't get away from the wallflower reputation she'd had all her life. That seemed to be all people remembered of her.

When she pulled up to the small cottage, Stephanie knew that she'd have to keep her mind occupied this weekend. Tomorrow after school, she needed to stop by the town library before they closed. A couple of long novels would do the trick. And maybe a big bag of popcorn and some chocolate chip cookies. Fortunately, weight had never been an issue for Stephanie. In fact, many people told her she was too skinny.

She spent the evening doing laundry and grading test papers. She was glad she had plenty to do at home; otherwise, she might go out of her mind thinking about Nathan Holloway and wondering what he was doing.

But Stephanie knew what Nathan was doing. He was spending time with his old college buddy, Ed Phillips, who was determined to put Nathan together with Pamela Pritchett.

As much as she hated to think this way, Stephanie didn't care for Pamela. She never had. Pamela had always put Stephanie down in ways that were very subtle, and she didn't have any defense other than saying something that would make her seem catty. So she'd kept her mouth shut and just put up with it.

In fact, the only time Stephanie ever felt like she had any special qualities was when Nathan Holloway was around. But after she'd overheard the comments Pamela had made in the hallway that morning, she figured she was delusional. He was only humoring her. What did he have to lose? After all, he was going right back to the glitz and glamor in New York, far, far away from Hartsville. He probably figured he could leave her with some memories for a lifetime.

But that wasn't what Stephanie wanted. Memories didn't keep her warm at night. Memories didn't make her feel special in the way that only the love of a good man could. And memories didn't keep her from wishing she could have something she could only dream about.

Yes, it was best if she kept her distance from Nathan Holloway.

Just when she was finishing her work, the phone rang. Stephanie's heart leaped, but she took a deep breath and answered it in her normal tone. It was Marla.

"Oh, it's you," she said without thinking.

"Why don't you at least try to sound happy to hear from me, Steph?" Marla said, her voice filled with its normal humor. "Don't you even want to know why I called?"

"Let's see," Stephanie said, rolling her eyes and

staring at the ceiling. "You want to tell me that what everyone's saying about me isn't true and that Nathan really likes me for myself rather than trying to do his good deed for the year."

"You're a mind reader, Steph."

"No, I just think you're doing what any good friend would do to make me feel good."

"Listen to me, Steph," Marla said. "I've got it from a good source that Nathan really likes being with you."

"Who?" Stephanie asked, doing her best to keep her hopes in check. The last thing she needed was to think she had a chance when she was better off just not thinking about it. "Who's the source?"

"Nathan, himself."

"Nathan said that?" Stephanie shrieked. Her heart started pounding so hard Stephanie was sure Marla could hear it over the phone.

"Well," Marla said, dragging out the one-syllable word. "Not exactly in those words."

"What exactly did he say?" It was impossible for Stephanie to keep the excitement from her voice. She really wanted to know.

"Exact words?"

"Exact words."

"He said he didn't want to hurt you."

Stephanie's heart fell with a thud. "That's not the same thing as liking to be with me, Marla."

"You had to be there."

"Look," Stephanie said as she held out her hand and inspected her nails. "I appreciate what you're trying to do, but give it up. I know my station in life here in Hartsville. If I think I have a chance with Nathan Holloway, I'm playing out of my league. I'm much better off leaving him to people like Pamela Pritchett."

"But he doesn't like Pamela," Marla argued.

"You don't know that. Besides, Ed, er, Mr. Phillips is determined to get the two of them together. Who am I to stand in the way?"

"Really, Stephanie, you give up way too easily. I'd never let someone do that to me."

"Trust me on this, Marla. It's for the best."

"Okay, okay, I'll give it up. But promise me you won't turn your back on Nathan if he tries to talk to you. I know how your pride works, and he might have something nifty to say."

"Something nifty?" Stephanie had to laugh at her friend's choice of words. Only Marla would say something like that.

"Promise?"

"Promise."

"Good, then, now that that's settled, how about going to a movie and the Dairy Swirl tomorrow night?"

"I'm busy," Stephanie answered.

"Doing what?"

"I've got things to do. You know, like catch up on my reading and get some rest."

"Sounds like a blast," Marla said, her disappointment obvious. "If you change your mind, you can always call me or let me know tomorrow in school."

Stephanie finally got to bed. But she couldn't go to sleep right away. As she lay there looking up at the ceiling, all sorts of images passed through her mind. Images of Nathan and herself dancing at Mr. Phillips's house. Images of Pamela Pritchett standing at the edge of the room and pretending she was having fun. Images of Nathan and Pamela gazing into each other's eyes. Sometime much later she dozed off.

Morning came much too early. It was time to go to school and face everyone who already knew about the intimate little dinner party where Pamela and Nathan would be together. And everyone seemed to think they were the perfect match.

Nathan didn't show up for his first appointment.

Mr. Phillips came to Stephanie's classroom and crooked his finger, motioning for her to come out to the hall and talk to him. She excused herself from the class and did as she was told.

"Have you seen Nathan?" Mr. Phillips got straight to the point. He didn't hold any punches.

Stephanie slowly shook her head. "No, not today. Why?"

"He didn't show up to take pictures, and I thought you might know where he is."

"Did you ask Miss Pritchett?" Stephanie couldn't resist.

"No," he replied, distracted by a thought. "I guess I should ask her next."

"Have you tried calling his hotel room?"

"Good idea," Mr. Phillips said. "I'll do that first. No need to alarm Miss Pritchett. After all, the two of them have a date tomorrow night. Nathan sure is looking forward to it."

"Yes, I've heard," Stephanie said, her focus turning to the floor tiles.

Mr. Phillips leaned toward her and patted her on the shoulder. "Don't take it so hard, Miss Mansfield. Nathan always was the ladies' man. I remember women dropping at his feet like flies back in college."

"I can imagine."

"Go back to your students now. I'll call the hotel."

She stood there and watched Mr. Phillips walk away and head toward the office. Then, she took three deep breaths before returning to her students.

No matter how hard Stephanie tried, she couldn't get her mind off that conversation with Mr. Phillips all morning. Her students kept looking at her funny, but she was distracted. Where *was* Nathan?

Chapter Five

Stephanie dismissed her students when the lunch bell rang before she gathered her teaching materials and filed them in the drawer. She grabbed her purse and headed for the cafeteria, resisting the temptation to stop by the makeshift photography room.

Nathan was a big boy, and with Mr. Phillips looking for him, Stephanie didn't worry. Besides, Hartsville was a small town. He couldn't have gone far.

The teachers' line in the cafeteria had already formed and was rather long by the time she got there. Marla was up toward the front, so Stephanie pretended not to see her. She didn't feel like talking to anyone right now.

She thought she'd gotten away with it, but as soon as she had her lunch and started heading toward her classroom, Marla reached out and grabbed her arm from behind. "Stephanie, we need to talk."

"If it's about Nathan, I'd rather not, if you don't mind."

"It *is* about Nathan, and I *do* mind."

Stephanie let out a deep sigh. "Okay, Marla, what is it?"

"Nathan stopped by my house last night."

"He what?" Already Stephanie's ears were ringing.

"You heard me. He needed to talk."

Stephanie felt her face grow hot. She was certain Marla could read her mind—that she was dying to hear what he had to say. But she couldn't ask.

"Do you know where he is?" Stephanie squeaked.

"Of course I do. That's what I wanted to talk to you about."

Another sigh. "Okay, spill it, Marla." She wasn't going to do this, but right now she couldn't resist.

"He's at your place."

"My place? But why?"

Marla chuckled softly. "He wanted to capture the view from the ridge in the morning sun. I told him I'd let Mr. Phillips know he'd be a few hours late."

"Then why—?" Stephanie began before she was interrupted.

"I have no idea why Mr. Phillips felt like he had to come and ask you where Nathan was. I told him first thing this morning, and he wanted to know if you were at school."

Stephanie felt the heat from Marla's gaze as she glanced down at her feet. She knew why Mr. Phillips wanted to talk to her. It was obvious. He wanted to make sure she wasn't up to something so he could steer Nathan toward Pamela Pritchett or one of the other Hartsville beauty queens.

Marla reached out and touched Stephanie's arm. "This isn't right, Steph. You and Nathan have the right to be with whomever you want to be with, but unfortunately, Hartsville is a small town where everyone tries to fit in their little groove. Too bad the tiny cracks started in junior high school turn out to determine our future groove."

That was something Marla and Stephanie had talked about many times—how people made their way when they were barely teenagers. And the social caste they entered then became more and more concrete as time went on. Nothing had changed. Pamela Pritchett was "in," and Stephanie Mansfield was an outsider.

"It's none of my business, Marla. What goes on between Nathan and Pamela, even if it's Mr. Phillips who does the matchmaking, is something I don't need to worry about."

Marla shook her head as a look of concern crossed her face. Stephanie knew she had a good friend here—one who really cared about her. "You don't need to worry about it, but you do need to stand up for yourself."

"I'll be okay. Really."

Stephanie began to turn toward her classroom when she spotted someone coming down the hall. She quickly glanced up. It was Nathan.

As soon as their gaze met, a huge, lazy, lopsided grin covered his face. "Hi, there, Stephanie." He nodded toward Marla. "Marla."

"Were your ears burning?" Marla said. Stephanie wanted to kick her, but she didn't. She just stood there with a stupid smile on her lips.

"No, why?" he asked as he stopped and turned toward them. "Were you talking about me?"

"Everyone is," Marla answered.

Why didn't she keep her mouth shut before she said something embarrassing? Stephanie would have to have a talk with her later about that.

He chuckled. "I hope you didn't forget to tell Ed I'd be late."

"No," Marla said as she turned to wink at Stephanie. There she went again. "I told him."

"Since he made the schedule pretty loose, I knew it would be easy to catch up and get everyone in this afternoon," Nathan said, looking suspiciously back and forth between Marla and Stephanie, like he thought they might be keeping something from him.

"I think he wanted to wait and see when you'd get back," Marla replied. "He's in the office now. Why don't you go talk to him?"

"I'll do that, but first I'd like to chat with "Stephanie."

Nathan glanced at Marla, who retreated with a knowing smile.

As soon as she was gone, Nathan turned to Stephanie. "I got the most incredible pictures on your property this morning. The sunlight filtered through the trees, giving the whole place a surreal look that reminds me of heaven."

Stephanie laughed. "My place looks like your concept of heaven?"

He shuffled his feet and thrust his hands in his pockets. "Well, yeah, sort of."

"I like it." Stephanie really did like her property. In fact, she loved it. She knew what he meant by the lighting.

Early in the morning, before the sun rose above the trees, it cast rays between the leaves that filtered it before it reached the ground. Even as a little girl, Stephanie found comfort in that, knowing that regardless of anything else that happened in Hartsville, she had her very own special place where she could go and feel downright regal. In fact, that was one of the main reasons she didn't want to leave. Her grandmother had created something that she truly cared about.

"What was going on with Marla?" he asked.

Stephanie shrugged. "I'm not sure, but I do think you need to go talk to Mr. Phillips. He came to see me this morning."

He cocked his head to one side. "Didn't Marla tell him where I was?"

She nodded. "That's what she told me, but he came and asked if I'd seen you."

Nathan narrowed his eyes and a look crossed his face that confused her. For the first time since she'd met him, he actually looked angry.

"I'll go talk to him now," Nathan said, backing away from Stephanie. He looked at her and wondered what was on her mind. She looked confused.

As Stephanie turned and walked back to her classroom, he noticed her slumped shoulders and look of resignation on her face. Hartsville wasn't good to her. And much to his disappointment, Ed Phillips was part of the problem. Nathan didn't like that one single bit.

He was determined to change things before he left. Generally, it wasn't in Nathan's nature to try to change anything. He went about his business and expected everyone else to do the same. But he cared about Stephanie Mansfield. She was truly a good person. And although looks weren't the most important thing in everyday life, he wasn't kidding when he'd told Ed he thought she was beautiful.

First, he'd have to come up with a plan. Since he didn't know most of the people beyond their names and what they did for a living, he figured he'd have to depend on someone else, like Marla. She was a good friend to Stephanie, and he could tell that she didn't like the treatment everyone was giving her, either.

That afternoon he finished all his photography a little later than usual. He was afraid he'd miss Marla before she left for the day, so he carefully put his camera away and tossed everything else in the carrier. Then he literally ran to Marla's class, only to find her with her head over a stack of papers on her desk. She glanced up when he cleared his throat.

Her eyebrows shot up, then her face softened when she saw who it was. "Hi, Nathan. What can I do for you?"

"Do you have a minute?" he asked as he walked into the classroom toward her desk.

"Sure," she replied, putting her red pen down and leaning toward him. He liked the fact that she was willing to give him her undivided attention.

"It's about Stephanie," he began.

"I figured that much."

"I hope you don't mind."

Marla shook her head. "No, I don't mind at all."

Nathan inhaled deeply and let his breath out slowly so he could collect his thoughts. Then he told her his feelings, and she listened with rapt attention.

"Well, Nathan, you've only been here a little while, and you have this whole town pegged."

"So I'm right?" he said as he pulled away from the tiny desk he'd been leaning against.

"Are you ever!"

"I want to do something, Marla."

He studied her as she drummed her fingers on the desk and thought for a moment. "Do you have anything in mind?"

Nathan shrugged and held his hands out. He had no idea what to do, but he wanted to make Stephanie feel special. "I was hoping you'd have some suggestions."

Her eyes twinkled, and she nodded as she grinned back at him. "I might have a few. Can you stick around for a little while so I can grade these papers before the weekend?"

"Sure," he said. "I need to do some work to finish with the pictures, anyway."

Nathan headed back to the room where his equipment was stashed. He really didn't have anything pressing that needed to be taken care of, but he figured he might as well find something to do. So he pulled everything out of the bag and repacked it neatly.

Just as he was about to zip the bag, Ed came into the room. "Looking forward to Saturday night, Nathan?"

Nathan shrugged. He wasn't happy with his old friend at the moment.

Ed came closer and looked around at all the equipment that needed to be stored over the weekend. "Need some help with that?"

"I suppose I could use an extra hand."

They found a spot for the equipment in Ed's office. Since it took them two trips each, Nathan was comfortable not talking until they were finished.

Finally, Ed laughed out loud. "I don't know what's eating at you, but I'm sure you'll snap out of it by tomorrow. Pamela is really thrilled to be your date for the evening."

Nathan looked up at Ed and shook his head. Ed just didn't seem to get it. "I could have found my own date."

Ed nodded, and Nathan wanted to rip that stupid grin right off his face. "Yeah, but you seem to have a soft spot in your heart for homely women who latch on to you, Nathan, old buddy."

No, Ed didn't get it.

"Why don't you come home with me this afternoon, and we can have a drink and unwind?" Ed said.

"No, sorry, Ed, but I've got other plans."

Ed's eyebrows shot up. "Pamela Pritchett?"

"No." He couldn't look his friend in the eye.

"Don't tell me you're seeing Miss Mansfield again."

"No."

Slowly a grin eased across Ed's face as he reached over and slapped Nathan on the back. "You sly dog. You've been out scouting your own women. I have to hand it to you, buddy. You've never had a hard time in the female department. Who is it?"

"It's none of your business, Ed."

"Why?" Ed asked, clearly stunned by Nathan's blunt reply. "Is she married?"

Nathan nodded. "Something like that."

"Uh, Nathan, I don't know what you do in New York, but here in Hartsville, we don't take kindly to that sort of thing."

"Relax, Ed," Nathan said, glad he'd finally gotten through to his old friend. He had a conscience at least. "She and I are friends. We're just going to chat."

"Be careful," Ed said. "You know that even innocent relationships can look pretty guilty."

"Yes," Nathan said with a chuckle. "I know."

"Well, okay, then," Ed finally conceded. He pulled a slip of paper from his pocket. "Here's Pamela's phone number. Call her and make arrangements to pick her up tomorrow."

Nathan took the paper and nodded. For some odd reason, he'd thought he'd be meeting Pamela Pritchett at Ed's house rather than having to pick her up like it was a real date. He should have known better.

Mr. Phillips was gone for a few minutes before Marla showed up at his door. "Wanna go somewhere so we can talk?" she asked.

"Sure."

"How about my house? My husband will be home in about a half hour, and you can meet him. I have a feeling the two of you will hit it off."

"Sounds good."

Nathan followed Marla to her neat little clapboard house in a quiet neighborhood with tree-lined streets. The lawns were green, and each home seemed to have at least one big tree in the front yard. His heart twisted at the feeling he had at something so basic. This was what was pictured as the perfect family home on television shows and in magazine ads.

"I haven't had a chance to clean this place in a while," Marla apologized as they went in the front door and made their way back to the bright, cheery kitchen.

It looked perfectly fine to Nathan. In fact, nothing was out of place, and it smelled nice, kind of like cut flowers. It was a little dark at first, but as Marla walked through the house, she opened the blinds and curtains, bringing what little outside light there was into the house.

"Something to drink?" she asked. "I've got iced tea, lemonade, and some diet soda." She'd already opened the cupboard and pulled out two glasses.

"Sure," he answered. "Whatever you have."

They sat down at the table with their drinks and just stared at each other for a moment, making Nathan a little uncomfortable. Finally, Marla spoke.

"Looks like Mr. Phillips is really pushing you toward Miss Hartsville."

"Miss Hartsville?" Did he miss something?

She tossed her hair over her shoulder and laughed. "Sorry. That's what Hank and I call Pamela when we discuss the people from this wonderful town."

"Oh, I see." Nathan studied his iced tea glass and wondered how to bring up the questions he wanted answers to. Questions about Stephanie.

"So are you looking forward to your date tomorrow night?"

One side of his mouth lifted in a sardonic grin as he nodded. Nothing got past the people of this town. Everyone knew everyone else's business.

"Sorry to be so nosy, but everyone's talking about it."

"That's okay," he finally said. "At least you're being open about it."

"Yeah," she said. "I tend to be that way. Open Marla."

A car pulled into the driveway, and Marla glanced up, her eyes lit with happiness. "Hank's home."

The sight of the love in Marla's eyes when she announced her husband warmed Nathan's heart. Would any woman ever be that happy just to see him?

Sure, women cooed over him all the time, but he suspected that had a lot to do with the fact that their modeling futures depended a great deal on his photographic impression of them. If he'd been some average Joe on the street, would they have been so eager to please him?

Even though most of the teachers here in Hartsville fussed and fidgeted over their looks right before he snapped their pictures, he admired them for going back to their jobs of teaching children. They led real lives. Not just some image put before the public that could never be real.

"Nice to finally meet you, Nathan," Hank said as he pumped his hand. "Marla's been talking nonstop about the big-city photographer in town."

Nathan looked at Marla, whose face was bright red. She shrugged.

"I hope she's not saying bad things."

"No, of course not," Hank responded. "I hear all the ladies are smitten. Have you picked out a favorite one yet?"

Marla stepped up and took her husband's arm. "That's enough, Hank. I'm sure Nathan doesn't want to talk about those things."

Nathan looked back and forth between Marla and Hank and realized that they had something he hadn't even come close to. They had unconditional love and mutual respect, and regardless of the silly banter between them, their eyes sparked with emotion whenever they were in the same room.

"Hey, don't worry about it," Nathan said. "I actually do want to talk about it."

"Okay, I'm all ears," Hank said as he sat down at the table with his own glass of iced tea. He patted the spot next to him, looked at his wife, and said, "Sit down, honey. Nathan wants to talk."

Nathan sat down and started out letting them know that he hadn't planned to have a social life here in Hartsville, but it seemed Ed Phillips was determined for him to have one anyway. "I'm sure Miss Pritchett is very nice, but quite frankly, I'm not interested."

"Is there anyone you *are* interested in?" Marla asked. He could tell that she was fishing for something she already knew. Well, he'd just give her what she wanted.

"If I were to have a social life here, I'd probably want to share it with Stephanie. She seems very nice." He tried hard to keep the extent of his real feelings out of his voice, but he was afraid he hadn't succeeded.

"That's what I thought," Marla said, obviously pleased with his answer. "But Mr. Phillips doesn't like that idea, does he?"

"No," Nathan answered. "And I can't for the life of me figure out what his problem is."

Marla and Hank exchanged glances, and Nathan had a feeling he was about to learn something new. She turned to him and explained, in detail, the inner workings of life in a small town, where football games and homecoming were the highlight of every teenager's life. And once people grew up, they spent most of their time talking about their glory days.

"You've got to be kidding," he said. He knew it was something like this, but he didn't realize how deeply ingrained yet shallow the attitude was.

"No, I'm not kidding," Marla replied. "In fact, I don't think these people can even look at Stephanie and see her any differently than they did when she was ten years old and going through her awkward stage."

"That's too bad," Nathan said, his voice trailing off. And it *was* too bad.

"Yes, it is," Marla agreed. "And I'm glad someone else besides Hank and me can see something in her." A frown covered her face as she thought for a moment. "You're not going to be in town much longer, are you, Nathan?"

He shook his head no. "I'm afraid not. I have to get back to work early next week. This was supposed to be a vacation."

"Some vacation," she said.

Actually, it *was* a vacation. Being in Hartsville was such a change of pace for him, he felt refreshed. With the exception of the anguish he felt over what was happening to Stephanie, of course.

"Well, I think you should call Mr. Phillips and cancel your plans for tomorrow night," Marla said.

Hank spoke up this time. "No, honey, he can't do that. They're old friends, and there's sort of a code between guys about doing that kind of thing."

Marla rolled her eyes. "Guys. Who can figure them out?"

Both Hank and Nathan looked up at her and burst into laughter. Nathan really liked these two. In fact, he had a feeling he and Stephanie could be very good friends with them as a couple.

Where did that come from? Since when were he and Stephanie a couple?

Chapter Six

The thought slammed into Nathan's mind so hard he almost fell over. He'd only known Stephanie Mansfield such a short time, but he already cared for her. He cared whether or not she was accepted. He cared whether or not she was happy. He cared about being with her more than he thought he'd ever want to be with anyone.

That wasn't like him at all. Well, at least it hadn't been after Jennifer, supermodel extraordinaire, had dumped him for her leading man in the first movie she ever starred in. He'd vowed immediately after Jennifer rushed into another man's arms that he'd never allow his heart to get soft again.

And he hadn't.

Until now.

Nathan knew right then and there that it was time for him to return to New York where he could get lost among the throngs of people and buildings that majestically towered over everyone, showing all its subjects how powerless they actually were in the overall scheme of things. Yes, he'd pack up his things and head home as soon as he finished what he'd obligated himself to do.

With a sigh of relief, Nathan turned to Marla and Hank and said, "I don't like the way Stephanie's being treated, but she's a grown woman. She can take care of herself. Besides, if she's really miserable, she has the option of leaving. I'm sure there are many other places where she can teach, if she's good."

Marla narrowed her eyes as if she was confused. Nathan understood that. He'd just taken an about-face on his attitude. But he had to. It was a matter of self-preservation. If he didn't harden up just a little—well, maybe a lot—he'd have to deal with feelings later. His own feelings. Feelings of caring about someone so much he'd lose part of his purpose in life—to become the best and most sought-after photographer in the world. He was well on his way. *Can't stop now,* he thought to himself.

"Okay," Marla said slowly, never taking her gaze off Nathan.

Hank nodded. He knew what was going on without having to be told.

"Well, better get outta here," Nathan said as he

backed toward the door. "Thanks for the tea and hospitality."

Marla stood at the door and watched him, a look of confusion on her face. He knew Hank would explain it to her after he was gone, which suited him just fine. The last thing Nathan needed was to have to make explanations about his every move.

He headed to his hotel so he could get some rest. He had a few things to think about, and he wanted to watch a show on television. At least it should be a quiet evening.

But it wasn't. By the time he got to his room, the light was blinking on the telephone, and when he checked his messages, there were a half dozen calls. Two from Pamela Pritchett, one from another teacher at the school, and three from Ed Phillips, each one sounding more urgent than the one before.

"Call me as soon as you get in, Nathan. I don't know where you are, but it can't be far. This town isn't that big." Click.

Nathan shut his eyes, rubbed his forehead, and blew out a few deep breaths. He had to call Ed back, even if it meant possibly giving up a night of solitude and mental rest.

Ed answered on the first ring. "Good. You're in. I'll be by in a half hour."

"Uh, Ed, I thought I'd just hang out here tonight."

"Nonsense. You're leaving next week, and I don't know when I'll ever get you back to Hartsville."

"What do you have in mind?" Nathan asked as he looked longingly at the television.

"Well," Ed began, a chuckle shaking his voice, "I just happen to know one very pretty lady who doesn't have anything to do tonight."

"I take it you're talking about Miss Pritchett." Oh, man, that was the last thing he needed.

"Good guess."

"I can't."

"You can't?" Ed squeaked.

"Uh, no," Nathan replied. "I kind of, uh, have a date." His mind reeled as he tried to think of something else, but he came up blank.

"I don't suppose you're talking about Miss Mansfield," Ed said in a monotone.

"You guessed it."

"But I thought you didn't have plans," Ed said sarcastically.

Nathan had to think fast. "I was going to rest for a little while and then ride out to see Stephanie."

"Do you have to?" Ed sounded desperate. He must have made some hefty promises to Miss Pritchett.

"She *is* expecting me," Nathan said, wishing he hadn't gotten himself in so deep. That's what he got for returning his calls.

"Well," Ed said, drawing out the single-syllable word. "I guess if you have an obligation, you have to honor it. After all, you're a decent guy."

If he only knew, Nathan thought. He wasn't sure

what else he said, but he was anxious to get off the phone as fast as he could.

The instant he hung up, he dug through his papers for Stephanie's phone number. He had to call to make sure she knew he was coming. After all, if Ed took it upon himself to check up on him, he didn't want to come across as a liar.

"I'm just sitting here reading a book," Stephanie said. She sounded distant, but he couldn't let that sway him.

"Do you mind if I stop by?"

"You want to come here?" she asked as if she didn't believe him.

"Yeah," he replied. "I feel like taking a drive, and I thought you might want to go with me."

"Well," she said, hesitating an uncomfortable few seconds. "I guess that would be fine. When are you leaving?"

"In about fifteen minutes."

"That should put you here in about a half hour. I'll be ready," she said, her voice now sounding more upbeat.

Hadn't it only been an hour ago he'd decided against getting any more involved with Stephanie than he already was? Nathan dazedly hung up the phone.

But what choice did he have? Ed had called, and he couldn't think of anything else to do. If he'd said one thing and done another, he surely would have been caught in this small town. So he *had* to go to Stephanie's house. He had no choice.

Nathan took a few extra minutes to psyche himself up for another get-together with Stephanie. He had to plant in his own mind the seed of doubt about his feelings for her. He needed to present reasons for keeping his heart inside his chest rather than letting her touch it so he could go back to New York and resume life as usual.

The drive out to Stephanie's house was incredible. Each mile brought new scenery, and each minute dropped the sun measurably into the horizon, turning the sky all shades of blue and pink and everything in between. It was heart-stopping.

At one point, Nathan had to pull the car off the road and just stop to stare. His camera was lying on the seat next to him in the car. He knew that if he started taking pictures, he might not finish until the sun disappeared completely. Still, though, it was tempting.

"Better get going," he mumbled to himself as he started his car.

The drive to Stephanie's property was so beautiful he could easily have lost himself in just staring out the window. But instead, he needed to focus on the issue at hand. Ed was trying to fix him up with Pamela Pritchett, and Nathan didn't want to be fixed up with anyone. Yet he was heading out to the house of the only woman in Hartsville who had managed to touch his heart. How smart was that?

Several times Nathan thought about turning around and heading back to the hotel and calling Stephanie. Surely she'd understand if he'd suddenly come down with a headache and needed to rest. But he couldn't do that to her, just like he couldn't lead Pamela Pritchett on by spending too much time with her.

By the time Nathan pulled into the long driveway that led to Stephanie's house, he could have been truthful with the headache excuse. But the instant he saw the house, he knew how badly he wanted to see her. His heart had begun pounding, and his senses were all more attuned. The visual images were sharper, and his ears could hear every leaf as it rustled in the trees.

Stephanie walked out onto the porch just as he turned off his engine. The sight of her silhouetted against the white cottage, the sun behind him casting incredible shadows over the land, presented such a surreal picture his mind totally went blank. It was almost as if he'd stepped onto the set of a movie where nothing was real and everything was strictly for the sake of the story. And his heart almost reached out to the woman he couldn't stop staring at.

Her face lit up when he stepped out of the car. "Nathan," she whispered softly.

Nathan gulped. "Hi, Steph." He tried his best to

sound casual and nonchalant, but it was growing increasingly more difficult with each second.

Stephanie tilted her head to one side and looked at him questioningly. "Did you want to come inside for a few minutes, or would you like to go for a drive now?"

Nathan stopped in his tracks. Which would be safer? Go inside or drive somewhere out in the open country? Each held danger for his heart at the moment.

"Uh, let's go for a drive," he said, sounding way too much like a juvenile on his first date.

"Great!" she said, meeting him in the yard, tossing her sweater over her shoulder. "Let's go."

"You're ready?"

Stephanie nodded.

Didn't most women take forever to get ready? Stephanie headed right for his car and started to open it before he could get there to do it for her. She hesitated for a second and just looked at him.

"Nathan, are you all right?"

He took advantage of her hesitation and rushed to her side. "I'm fine. It's just that I didn't expect you to be outside."

She grinned as she slid effortlessly into the passenger seat.

"I guess I'm just eager to get away," she said. "I'm really glad you called, Nathan."

He felt guilty. He hadn't wanted to come. Well, he'd wanted to, but he knew it wasn't for the best.

Without looking directly at Stephanie, he carefully said, "I thought this might be kind of nice on my last weekend here."

She looked at him for a moment before softly saying, "And you have a date tomorrow night with Pamela."

The instant that left her mouth, Stephanie wished she'd stopped before she'd said so much. So far, she'd managed to remain cool, calm, and collected. Letting him know how she felt wasn't acceptable right now, especially since he'd be leaving in a few days.

She needed to remain calm. She needed to keep her emotional distance.

Stephanie pulled her hands into her lap and began to fidget with the edge of her sweater. She didn't know what else to do, now that they were sitting alone in his car.

"Music?" he asked as he reached over and opened the glove compartment. "I brought some tapes."

She nodded. At least music would get her mind off her feelings.

Since he'd put both hands back on the steering wheel, obviously he expected her to pick something to play. She chose something with a lively beat.

Everything else had too much potential to get to her emotions.

When Stephanie glanced up from the tape player, the view before her caught her breath. She looked over at Nathan and saw that it had affected him the same way.

"Pull over," she said softly.

He did exactly what she told him to do, no argument. Pulling out his camera and strapping on the long handle, he added, "I hope you don't mind if I—"

She interrupted. "No, I don't mind if you take pictures. In fact I wish I'd brought my own camera."

Stephanie stood by Nathan's car and watched as Nathan snapped shots of the sun sinking behind the trees, moving around to a different spot to capture the image of a lone tree in a clearing, appearing as an oasis to a flock of birds who'd chosen it to homestead, and then angling back to include her in some of the shots.

"You don't want me in your pictures," Stephanie said self-consciously.

For the first time in many minutes, he stopped shooting pictures and looked directly at her without the camera between them. "And why not?"

She shrugged. "It'll ruin the scenery. You need pictures of the countryside."

"Come on, Steph," he said, snapping one picture

after another while she blushed and moved around self-consciously. Why was he doing this?

Stephanie had to admit, she felt special whenever Nathan was around, especially when he had his camera pointed at her. He had a way of making her feel beautiful. Of having something no one else saw.

After about five minutes of snapping pictures, he stopped, put the lens cover on the camera, and said, "Okay, let's go."

Just like that. *Let's go*. No asking her what she wanted. No transition from snapping pictures. Just *let's go*.

Nathan stared at her in wonder. She really didn't have any idea what kind of impact she had on him. And although it was better that way, he felt like she should have had some inkling of what she was doing to his heart.

And his mind.

Ever since he'd met her, he hadn't been able to think straight. In fact, he'd actually had thoughts of falling in love. Settling down. Maybe even bringing a child or two into the world. He *knew* he was losing his mind.

Any man in this world who had all the things going for him that Nathan had wouldn't even think such thoughts. No, he should be concentrating on his next big account, the international cosmetics company that hired him to do the European photo shoot next month.

Maybe he'd get over such nonsensical thoughts once he was surrounded by all those gorgeous models.

"Nathan," Stephanie said softly.

He made the huge mistake of turning and looking directly into her eyes. His heart leaped. Those European models didn't have anything over the woman who sat in the passenger seat right next to him now.

"What?" he asked huskily.

"Where are we going?"

"Uh," he began. He had to rack his brain to think of something, then he said, "Dairy Swirl."

"Dairy Swirl?"

Nathan nodded. "I thought that might be fun."

She smiled. "Yes, it can be fun. I like ice cream."

Stephanie was so gorgeous when she smiled, her generous mouth lighting up the inside of the car that had begun to grow dark with the approaching evening.

"I thought it might bring back some memories."

Suddenly, the smile faded. "The food's good, but the memories I could do without."

Nathan was puzzled. He thought the Dairy Swirl was the teen hangout of Hartsville. "But I thought—"

He stopped when she began to shake her head. "No, the Dairy Swirl was the place to be seen if you were part of the in crowd."

Nathan hadn't heard that expression in quite some time. "The in crowd?"

"You know, the popular kids?" She shrugged and shook her head, only glancing at him for an instant. Then she quickly looked away. Someone had really done a number on this woman's psyche. Did Pamela Pritchett reign as beauty queen of Hartsville just because she looked good as a teenager?

While Pamela had some nice features—a cute little upturned nose, pretty bow-shaped lips that had thinned with age, and big, round blue eyes—Stephanie looked downright regal. She had nice long shapely legs, chiseled features, and a complexion most models would sell their souls for.

Stephanie had obviously opted for the natural look, while Pamela had done everything in her power to hold onto her youth. And it had the reverse effect. Her bleached blond hair was definitely over-processed, and her skin had been tanned so much it looked like leather.

Another question that was nagging at the back of Nathan's mind was what part in this personal blow to Stephanie's ego did his friend Ed play? Did Ed contribute to her lack of self-esteem? It certainly seemed like it from Nathan's vantage point.

The more Nathan thought about how Ed acted back in college, the more he was reminded of little things that didn't seem all that significant at the time. Like the time Nathan had invited a girl to a campus concert and Ed had cold-shouldered her just because she wasn't wearing the "right" clothes. Nathan had just laughed it off as a joke.

Now he realized it was the way Ed thought. Small-town mentality. Narrow-minded. But not everyone in this town was like that, Nathan had noticed. Stephanie and Marla and . . . well, there were a few others, but he couldn't think of them right off the top of his head. The one who frustrated him most was Ed.

No sense in getting angry at Ed now, Nathan thought. But it was hard.

What he still had a hard time figuring out was why Stephanie had returned to teach in such a repressive environment. She could have gone anywhere else and been much happier. There must have been a good reason; she was a smart woman.

"Nathan?" she said, breaking his train of thought. Good thing, because he was beginning to get angry with everyone in Hartsville but Stephanie.

"Yes?"

"Did I say something to offend you?"

Yes, but not about anything you did, he wanted to say. But he didn't. Instead, he forced a smile and replied, "No, I was just thinking about how long it's been since I've had ice cream."

"Well, you're in for a real treat," she said on the edge of a snicker. "It's typical soft-serve with plenty of ice crystals, discoloration, and cones that can't hold it until you're finished with the ice cream. I can almost guarantee it'll melt all over you before you're halfway finished."

"Mmm," he said. "Sounds good."

She nodded. "It is."

When Nathan pulled in front of the Dairy Swirl, he couldn't help but notice there were very few cars in the parking lot. "Where is everyone? It's Friday night. I expected it to be packed with kids."

"They're not finished cruising yet," Stephanie answered as she opened her door and got out.

He followed her inside. "Cruising?"

"Yeah. That's what the very bored teenagers of Hartsville do on Friday and Saturday night. They cruise by one another's houses and honk. Then, they form a caravan and drive around some more, and they generally wind up here by the end of the night. If we stick around long enough, we might even get to see some of the action."

"Sounds exciting," he said with a smirk.

"Trust me, it's nothing compared to what you're probably used to in New York. But for Hartsville, it's all we've got."

Nathan didn't tell her what he was thinking—that his exciting Friday nights were generally spent locked in the darkroom of his apartment in the high-rise building where he'd lived for the past seven years. The only time he came out was when his stomach rumbled and after there was nothing left for him to do, which was generally sometime after midnight.

The Dairy Swirl was definitely more exciting for him than Friday nights in New York. And what made it especially nice was having Stephanie by his side.

"I'm having a hamburger," he said. "You want dinner?"

She crinkled her nose. "I had a grilled cheese sandwich when I got home from school. I'll wait for you to have dessert."

Without even asking, he got her a Coke to drink while he ate his dinner. The place was quiet and he and Stephanie had the place to themselves, while most of the customers came to the drive-thru.

Finally, he stood up and pointed to the menu board on the wall. "Now for dessert. What's the house specialty?"

Stephanie dramatically placed her finger on her chin and squinted her eyes, while her nose crinkled in that now-familiar way that charmed the socks right off his feet. "They have good banana splits, but I want something different."

"Okay, what'll you have?" he said. "Your wish is my command, dear maiden."

"In that case, I'll have the double hot-fudge sundae with the works." Her eyes sparkled in childlike glee.

The models he knew avoided dessert like the plague. He suspected some of them were closet sweets eaters, but he was almost positive none of them would ever have a double hot-fudge sundae with the works.

He ordered two of those from the young woman at the counter. She acted like it was normal as she turned around and repeated the order to the man standing by the ice cream machine. He went ahead and paid for it, and it was on the counter in a matter of minutes.

"Here ya go, Steph," Nathan said as he placed the delectable treat in front of her. Then he sat down and watched as she dipped her spoon into her bowl of ice cream and enjoyed it as if for the first time.

Nathan couldn't remember the last time he'd seen a New York woman eat with such reckless abandon, either. When they broke for lunch, he ate stale sandwiches while the models huddled in the corner and nibbled on carrots and drank bottled water.

"This is really great, Stephanie," he said after he'd taken a few bites.

She paused for a moment, holding her spoon in the air like a scepter. With a sticky smile, she nodded. "Yes, it is, isn't it?"

With a heart filled with more joy than he could ever remember having, Nathan dug in and heartily ate his own hot-fudge sundae. He thoroughly enjoyed every last bite.

"Wow!" she said when he finished.

"What?"

"You really, really liked that, didn't you?"

Nathan glanced down at his empty ice cream dish. "I must have."

Stephanie continued smiling as she went back to eating hers. She, too, finished her sundae, but she took her time savoring every last morsel.

She had just placed her spoon back in the dish when Nathan heard a familiar voice from behind. "I heard you were here, but I didn't believe it."

Chapter Seven

Nathan spun around and found himself face-to-face with Ed. "You heard I was here?"

Ed nodded as he sank down in the seat beside Stephanie. He turned and offered her an obligatory nod. "Miss Mansfield."

"Hi, Mr. Phillips," she said as her glance darted back and forth between Ed and Nathan. His heart went out to her.

Ed looked at Nathan. "This is a small town, Nathan. People like to talk."

Nathan chuckled. "Good thing I didn't want to hide."

"Yeah," Ed said. "You'd have to leave town to do that."

"It won't be long before I do just that," Nathan said.

These two men reminded Stephanie of a couple of bulls getting ready to charge each other, the way they were inhaling and exhaling through their noses. Why would there be so much tension between them? Weren't they best friends? That was what Mr. Phillips kept telling all the teachers when he told them that Nathan Holloway, famous world-class photographer, would be in town to take their pictures.

He'd made it sound like Nathan would do anything for him, including bend over backward and do double handsprings. It didn't look that way to her right now.

"So, Nathan, you looking forward to tomorrow night?" Ed said, acting like Stephanie wasn't even there. She wished she could just melt into the seat and disappear.

Nathan shrugged. "Sort of."

Why didn't they just stop acting like a couple of immature little boys? She felt like jumping up and running away, something she *would* do if they didn't quit this nonsense.

"I know Pamela's excited about her big date with the New York photographer," Ed said.

"Good." Nathan was clearly irritated. Why didn't he just tell Mr. Phillips he was with her and quit doing this rather than sending these stupid signals?

Mr. Phillips obviously couldn't take a hint. He kept talking. "In fact, I heard she was buying a brand-new dress and having it altered at the Petite Boutique, and that's not a cheap place to shop. I hope she gets something pink. She looks absolutely stunning in pink."

Nathan glared at Mr. Phillips. "Then why don't you ask her out yourself?"

Stephanie often wondered that herself. Mr. Phillips was single, and he clearly had a crush on Pamela. And she doubted Pamela would turn him down. After all, he'd been the "Big Man on Campus" way back when.

Mr. Phillips blushed—yes, he actually blushed—when he replied, "It wouldn't be right. After all, I'm the principal and she's one of my teachers."

Nathan chuckled. "That's ridiculous, Ed. You should be able to see whomever you want to."

Mr. Phillips shook his head. "Well, I'm not the one she's interested in anyway, Nathan. Ever since I made the announcement that you were coming to town, she started after me to somehow get the two of you together. And that's what I'm doing."

Stephanie sat there and watched the two men, amazed at how open Mr. Phillips was with Nathan. And in front of her, too! She would have been embarrassed to do something like this, especially when there was someone else present.

Finally, Nathan stood up. "Well, Ed, Stephanie and

I need to go. It sure was, er ... nice running into you."

"Good to see you, too, Nathan," Ed replied as he stood up and backed away. "Miss Mansfield, see you Monday."

The instant he left, Stephanie stood up beside Nathan, who had a look of irritation on his face. It seemed that whenever Mr. Phillips brought Pamela Pritchett into the conversation, Nathan had that same expression.

She didn't dare say anything. They went out to his car and got in before the silence was broken.

"I hate it when he does that," Nathan finally said when they got to his rental car.

"Does what?"

"Tries to fix me up with women."

"He's done this before?"

Nathan pounded the steering wheel. "He did it all the time back in college." Stephanie watched him go through one stage of anguish after another. "Naturally, I assumed he'd outgrown it, but he obviously hasn't."

"Outgrown it?"

Shaking his head and looking directly at her, Nathan replied, "Yes. Outgrown the need to live his life through me. I don't know what his problem is, but he seems to find happiness when I'm surrounded by women."

"And you don't?" she said with as much humor as she could muster.

"Not really," he replied, still studying her. "But I'm happy right now."

Stephanie felt her heart leap. But she knew better than to get her hopes up. She'd have too far to fall after Nathan went back to New York, and she still had to stay in Hartsville.

"Tell me something, Steph," he said as they crept along Main Street.

"Sure." She held her breath.

"Why do you stay here?" Nathan glanced over at her, then focused back on the road. "I mean, I'm sure you could get a wonderful job teaching somewhere else. You could start over and make a name for yourself."

Her breath came out in a whoosh. "I can't do that."

"I see that," he said as he reached over and patted her hand. "But why not?"

Should she tell him? Or did it really matter? Was he just making conversation?

Oh well, she might as well spill her thoughts and reasons why she couldn't ever leave Hartsville. He'd be leaving soon, so it didn't really matter what he thought. Or did it?

"I promised my grandmother I'd stay," she blurted out.

"You what?"

"My grandmother," she repeated. "She raised me

in that house. When we found out she was sick, she told me how much she loved that place. I told her that I'd never leave. I'll always be there to take care of the house and the land she loved so much."

"But she's no longer here," he said. "Does it really matter?"

Stephanie nodded without hesitation. "To me it does."

She watched as Nathan processed this information. It was hard. She could tell. He didn't understand a pact made between a grandmother and granddaughter, probably because he'd never been that attached to his own grandparents.

"Besides," she continued, "Hartsville is really a nice town. Some of the people are kind of quirky, but I love teaching in the school where I went when I was a child."

Nathan nodded. "Seems like a nice school, but you can't seem to live down your reputation."

Stephanie chuckled. "I've always been considered the brainy one, but that's not so bad. People respect me, even if they don't think I'm cool."

Nathan kept glancing over at her, and she had to try hard to maintain her level head. It required quite a bit of concentration, but she managed to do it.

"Would you consider coming to New York sometime?" he asked.

She shrugged, trying hard to keep her composure, but it was growing increasingly difficult. "I might."

"I'd like for you to."

They remained silent most of the way back to her house, occasionally commenting on the colors of the foliage against the dark blue sky that was lit by the moon and all the stars. It was an exceptionally beautiful night.

When Nathan pulled into the driveway, Stephanie was torn between inviting him in and letting him just leave once she was inside. Either way, she felt that she'd have to deal with his absence once he left. But inviting him in would postpone the inevitable.

"Would you like to come in for something to drink?"

He hesitated for a moment, almost as if it were a major decision. Finally, he glanced at the illuminated face on his watch and shook his head. "Better not tonight, Steph. I had a long day, and Ed seems to have big plans for me tomorrow."

She sighed. This wasn't what she wanted to hear, but she accepted it. What choice did she have?

"I had a nice evening, Nathan," she said as she walked up the sidewalk.

He reached out and took both of her arms gently in his hands. "Steph," he said as he turned her around to face him.

She looked at him and saw something in his eyes that she couldn't decipher. It was an expression of confusion, but she had no idea what it was all about.

Nathan looked up at the sky, then back down at

her. Somehow, she knew she was about to be kissed. She should have stopped him, but she couldn't.

As his face came closer to hers, Stephanie had to decide what to do. It was a split-second decision.

Closing her eyes, she allowed his lips to touch hers, then she pulled back. As she gently pushed him away with her fingertips, she said with a shaky voice, "Nathan, I'd better go in."

He stood there and watched her as she ran inside. Stephanie knew he was watching because she could feel his gaze on her back. As soon as she got inside and turned on the lights, though, she heard his car engine start.

That was when she flopped over on the sofa and let the tears fall. No matter what happened, Stephanie knew she could never find true love as long as she remained in Hartsville. The place was filled with people who had a preconceived idea of how things should be. And if she ever tried to change that, she'd get verbally knocked down and ridiculed, just like she had back in junior high school when she thought she might have a chance with one of the boys who was considered a good catch.

Nathan had never been a violent man, but there were times when he could have put a hole through something with his fist. And this was one of those times.

Stephanie was amazingly relaxed and peaceful

through the whole ordeal with Ed at the Dairy Swirl, while his insides churned and his anger grew. What did Ed think he was doing, coming in like that and disrupting his time with Stephanie? He'd always thought Ed had more sense than that.

It was almost like Stephanie didn't deserve to be with him, it appeared. Was his old friend really a jerk, or was he just downright stupid?

Probably the latter. Even back in college, Ed stuck his foot in his mouth if he thought he could get something. But that was different. They were still young and could get away with being irresponsible.

Now, though, Ed was a principal of the elementary school. Stephanie's boss. Shouldn't he be more considerate of his employees?

And why was Stephanie taking such emotional abuse? He might be wrong, but it didn't look to him like she enjoyed any of it. Who would?

Maybe he should have a talk with Ed. Or maybe not. The last thing he'd want to do was make things more difficult for Stephanie after he left. After all, he didn't plan to return. Hartsville wasn't the kind of place that he planned to go to on vacation, although there were a few things he liked about it.

The downtown area was quaint and picturesque. He saw more photo opportunities than he took advantage of. People generally seemed to know one another, and they acknowledged friends on the street, often in a warm embrace. He liked seeing that.

The school felt safe, too. There were no bars on the windows or graffiti on the walls. Since everyone knew everyone else, strangers would have been noticed. If he had children, he'd want them to go to a school like that.

And the countryside was stunning, especially the area around Stephanie's house. Her property included a forest, a pond, and several acres of open field. The house was small, but that didn't matter. It fit.

One place Nathan did take quite a few pictures of was Stephanie's property. He couldn't help it, it was so beautiful. At least he'd have something to look at later, after he was back in New York. That would be enough of a reminder as to why he needed to stay away. As beautiful as the countryside was around Hartsville, he was a big-city kind of guy. He needed the lights and the action, not some little cottage out in the country.

When Ed had called and asked him to visit, Nathan thought at first that he meant a vacation out in the country, and it sounded like a nice change of pace. But by the end of the phone call, Nathan knew there was an ulterior motive—to take pictures of the teachers.

It didn't sound all that bad to him, though, because he figured it would be easy. The teachers would line up, he'd snap their pictures, and all he'd have to do at night would be hang around and watch television, read, and relax.

Sure, Ed offered him a place to stay, but Nathan didn't like doing that. He'd known Ed long enough to figure on a full social schedule, so he opted to stay in the only hotel in town. He was glad about that now. Staying with Ed would only have put him in a worse position with Pamela Pritchett.

Nathan knew that one of Ed's problems with Pamela was that he was so in love with her, he didn't know what to do with himself. And the small-town mentality of never changing stations in life kept him from making the moves he should have been making. Maybe Nathan could get him to rethink this attitude, but he wouldn't have bet his life on it, now that he'd seen how deep tradition was in Hartsville.

The night seemed much too long to suit Nathan. He found himself thinking about Stephanie, and he forced himself to replace her image with a mindless movie on late-night television. It was a B movie, but it didn't matter. It was something.

He had no idea when he'd fallen asleep, but he awoke feeling like he'd pulled an all-nighter. The TV was still blaring, and he was fully dressed.

With a groan, Nathan stood up, stretched, and headed for the bathroom. A nice cool shower sounded good to him right now. At least it would wake him up.

Ed called him right after he stepped out of the shower. "I've got some ideas for tonight, but I wanted to know what you thought."

"About what?" Nathan said as he towel dried his hair.

"Dinner tonight."

Nathan chuckled. Leave it to Ed to wait until the last minute to plan dinner. "I thought you mentioned something about steaks."

"Yeah, but I remembered that Pamela doesn't eat red meat."

"So have fish or chicken." Nathan felt his level of irritation rising, but he did his best to keep it out of his voice.

"Sure you don't mind?"

"Positive."

"Can you bring the wine?" Ed asked.

"I'll be glad to."

Ed cleared his throat. "Can you come early?"

"Sure, what time?"

"Maybe around four. I might need some help with dinner."

"Okay," Nathan replied, "but you need to let Miss Pritchett know she'll have to find another way there."

By the time Nathan got off the phone, he realized he'd just been manipulated into cooking dinner. *Oh well, that's too bad,* he thought. At least he only had a few more days left in Hartsville.

The very things he'd always thought funny about Ed Phillips were now a strong source of irritation for Nathan. Ed should have grown out of his lack of confidence to approach something new, including dinner and his attitude toward his old friends.

Then Nathan remembered the incident the night before with Stephanie. Ed sure hadn't taken her feelings into consideration when he just blurted out all the details about tonight with Pamela.

And Stephanie had just sat there, taking it all in, keeping her mouth shut like a nice little woman. That irritated him, too.

Face it, he thought. *Everything is irritating right now. It's time to get back to New York and try to put all this out of your mind.*

Nathan knew it wouldn't be easy to forget Stephanie, especially once he began to develop the pictures. He'd taken dozens of pictures of the teachers and hundreds of shots of the countryside, the town, and of Stephanie—some she was aware of and others when she wasn't looking.

But first he had to get through this date tonight, an entire Sunday, and a couple of days of make-up pictures for those teachers he hadn't gotten to yet. And he needed to do it with a good attitude.

Nathan spent most of the day walking around town, chatting with people who recognized him, and taking more pictures. There was a small historic monument in the center of the town square, which he studied and captured on film.

He spotted a group of children on a playground at

the edge of town a little later, and after getting permission from their caregivers, he snapped their pictures, too. Children were so oblivious to the world around them; that's what made them such wonderful subjects for candid shots.

Nathan kept a close eye on the time, since he'd made a commitment to Ed to help cook dinner. However, no matter what he did, his annoyance toward his friend still remained. Ed should never have stuck his neck out like he had, depending on Nathan to dig him out.

But that was nothing new. Back in college, it had happened many times. Nathan assumed Ed had grown up, especially since a few years had lapsed, Ed had taught school, and obviously gotten on the fast track to school administration. Now Nathan realized he must have pulled a few strings to have gotten where he was.

When it was time, Nathan packed up his equipment and headed back to the hotel. He'd planned on changing clothes, but the more he thought about it, the more he realized there was no reason. He was perfectly fine in his chinos and plaid shirt. If Pamela Pritchett didn't like it, then so what. He had no doubt Stephanie wouldn't have minded.

Nathan let out a long sigh. No matter what he did, what he tried to think about, Stephanie popped into his mind. The sooner he left the better. Maybe he could finish up on Monday and leave first thing Tuesday. He didn't think there would be a problem rescheduling his flight.

Stephanie curled up in the overstuffed chair she'd loved sitting in since she was a little girl. Her book lay facedown on the table, and she had plenty to drink and nibble on. She was set up for a marathon reading session, something she normally enjoyed.

But tonight was different. She couldn't seem to stop thinking about Nathan. Was he already at Mr. Phillips's house? Did Pamela finally get what she wanted? It wasn't too hard to figure out that Pamela wanted Nathan's attention, and she'd stop at nothing to get it.

Sure, everyone knew Ed Phillips was head-over-heels in love with the ex-beauty queen. But did Pamela care? Not on your life.

She used Ed's affection to get her way, whether it was to get a teaching job over someone who was much more qualified or doing whatever it took to get the attention of a New York photographer. In fact, she made it known all over town that she fully intended to make a name for herself and ditch the teaching profession.

She'd even told a bunch of people on the faculty at school that by the time Nathan Holloway left she'd have him eating out of her hand. No one seemed to doubt that she would, except for Marla, who'd pulled

Stephanie to the side and said, "She's such a dreamer. Just look at her."

"Isn't she the prettiest woman in Hartsville?" Stephanie had asked.

Marla snorted. "Maybe ten years ago, but not now. Besides, no one wants someone who's that stuck on herself."

Stephanie took it all in, but she knew that whatever Pamela wanted, Pamela generally got. At least it had been that way in the past. No reason to think that would end now.

With a sigh, Stephanie picked up her book. She'd better stop thinking about Nathan and Pamela, or it would be a very long, lonely night. *At least a book can't hurt you,* she told herself.

But no matter how many times she read the first paragraph, Stephanie couldn't get into the story. Even the strong hook of a murder didn't hold her attention.

Finally, she put the book down and picked up the remote control. Channel surfing wasn't something she normally enjoyed, but she did it now because none of the shows looked appealing. Her restlessness made her skin crawl.

Nothing worked. The book didn't hold her interest, the television shows seemed trite, and food had lost its taste. Stephanie finally had to face the fact that she was worried about what was going on between Nathan and Pamela.

Why she worried, she had no idea. There was absolutely nothing she could do about it. The whole thing was out of her control.

But still she worried. At some point, her interest in Nathan Holloway had gone beyond the mild curiosity everyone had about the famous photographer and progressed to genuine care and concern. She liked him. In fact, she liked him a lot.

Okay, he'd been at Ed's house for two hours and basically prepared the entire dinner. Ed had spent the whole time showering, changing clothes, and getting ready to see the women he'd invited over.

When Nathan had asked Ed if he'd been seeing the other person, one of Pamela's friends named Julie, for very long, Ed had almost bitten his head off. For no reason. Except he was in love with Pamela. Nathan could see it, Stephanie was aware of it, and Marla had let him know she suspected it, too. Why did Ed have to act so thick-skulled about where his heart was? He should have just come clean, started a relationship with the woman himself, and dared anyone to cross him. That's what Nathan would have done.

Well, wouldn't he? No one could tell him who to or not to date, right?

Obviously that wasn't the case. Here he was, cooking dinner for some woman he didn't want to be with, while the one he really wanted to see was at home doing who knew what.

Stephanie was quite a woman. She was smart, beautiful, and very caring. Her sweet nature was the direct opposite of what he dealt with all day while photographing temperamental models.

When Ed came into the kitchen reeking of cologne, Nathan cast him a sideways glance. "Trying to repel mosquitoes?"

Ed's face turned bright red. "Is it that strong?"

Nodding, Nathan suggested, "You'd better go wash some of it off, or no one will be able to smell this succulent roast chicken I prepared."

With a huge smile, Ed looked over Nathan's shoulder. "Thanks, pal. I owe you one."

"Yes, you do," Nathan agreed.

Ed's eyebrows shot up, and he took a defensive stance, his feet shoulder width apart, one arm folded over his chest, and the other elbow resting on his hand, his finger pointing up for emphasis. "But don't forget the fact that I fixed you up with the prettiest girl in Hartsville."

Nathan groaned. First of all, Pamela wasn't a girl, she was a woman. And secondly, she was by far *not* the prettiest female in Hartsville. But nothing he said would change Ed's opinion of Pamela Pritchett. His mind was made up, but he still couldn't read his own heart.

"Just go wash some of that smelly stuff off before they get here."

Nathan stood at the stove stirring the gravy as he watched Ed scamper out of the kitchen like a little kid. Three more days, and he'd be home. All he had to do was get through it.

Ten minutes later the doorbell rang. Ed had already returned to the kitchen, and he was hopping around all over the place, not sure what to do next.

"Answer the door!" Nathan ordered. *Man, this guy is a basket case!*

"Oh, okay," Ed said as he raced to the door like his life depended on it.

Nathan forced a smile when he spotted the two women who walked through the door.

They looked like color negatives of each other. Julie was as black-haired as Pamela was blond. Pamela wore a cotton-candy pink dress, while Julie was decked out all in shades of blue. His eyes ached if he looked at either one of them too long.

"Nathan Holloway," Julie gushed as she pumped his hand with both of hers. "I've heard so much about you. Pamela tells me you're only in town for a few more days. I hope you have time to stop by my office before you leave. I'm at Maverick Realty on Main Street."

"Oh, you're a realtor?" Nathan asked politely.

But Julie took it as an invitation to tell him all

about herself. "Oh, no, I'm just the secretary there. I don't think I'd be good at selling houses, but the agents tell me I have a nice phone voice. Maybe someday . . ." She went on and on, and at some point, Nathan stopped listening.

"Hey, girls," Ed said as he guided Julie and Pamela toward the dining room he'd set up with candles and a gaudy plastic centerpiece. "We've got a gourmet meal for you. Just sit back and relax while we serve you."

Both women giggled. Nathan cringed.

Ed never took his eyes off Pamela, while Julie went on and on about the real estate office. She must have discussed every single listing they had before they even sat down to eat.

"Ooh, this looks yummy!" Julie said, her voice squeaky and downright irritating.

Ed grinned at her and said, "Trust me, it is."

He never mentioned the fact that he hadn't lifted a finger in the kitchen other than to help bring the plates to the dining room.

"So tell me, Nathan," Pamela said as she leaned forward on her elbows. "How does someone like me get into modeling?"

Nathan almost choked on his chicken. He'd expected her to ask questions but not this early in the evening.

With a shrug he said, "It's pretty competitive, Miss

Pritchett. There are literally thousands of women vying for each modeling job. Are you sure you want to pursue something so difficult?"

"You have to admit, Nathan," Ed declared. "Most women don't have Pamela's natural beauty. I'll bet most women in New York would give up everything they have to look like her."

Nathan disagreed. But when he looked at Ed, all he saw was sincerity and genuine adoration. The man was so deeply in love with Pamela Pritchett nothing would make her look less than perfect in his eyes.

"Well, I suppose I can take a few shots so you can start a portfolio."

"Ooh," she cooed. "Would you do that for me?"

"Sure," he answered, wondering why he got himself into this situation.

"Oh, goodie!" Julie squeaked. "Can you take some pictures of me, too?"

Ed reached over and touched her arm sweetly. "I'm sure he wouldn't mind, Julie, honey, but don't get your hopes up. Not many people are in Pamela's league in the looks department."

Julie's face fell, but she quickly perked up when Nathan nodded. "While I've got the camera out, I might as well take a few of both of you." Then he turned to Ed. "Care to have your picture taken, too?"

Ed's hand went to his chest, and his face reddened. "Me? Why, sure. I'll be glad to help you finish out a roll of film."

All through the rest of the meal, Julie, Pamela, and Ed were so excited they couldn't finish a complete thread of conversation. And Nathan wished he was anywhere else but here.

Since Julie and Pamela were so excited about getting their pictures taken, Ed shooed them off to fix themselves up while he and Nathan cleaned up the kitchen.

As soon as they were gone, he turned to Nathan and said, "You just made some major points with Pamela, old pal. She really likes you."

Nathan snorted. "It's not me she likes. It's my camera."

Ed's eyes almost bugged out of his head. "Pamela's not like that. Why, she's the sweetest and most sincere person I know."

Oh, that's right. He's in love with the woman, Nathan thought. *Rule Number One: Don't insult a woman to the man who loves her.*

"I'm sure she is," Nathan replied.

"We're ready," Julie called from the living room. "Where would you like us to pose?"

Chapter Eight

Nathan blew out a deep breath he'd been holding. Time to go to work.

He went out to his car and got the camera that went everywhere with him. This was one time he wished he'd left it at the hotel.

By the time he got back to everyone, they were all lined up on the sofa, looking straight ahead with their hands folded in their laps. They looked downright comical.

"We're ready, Nathan," Ed said. "Where do you want us to sit?"

I don't want you to sit, he felt like telling his old friend. *I want to be able to have dinner with friends and relax like everyone else seems to be able to do. I want to feel like I feel when I'm with Stephanie.*

"Why don't you each get up, one at a time, and I'll try to position you and give you a little direction," Nathan said, contradicting his thoughts.

Pamela gently shoved Julie off the sofa. "Why don't you go first? I have a feeling I'll be posing longer, and I don't want to keep you from having fun."

Nathan shuddered. Pamela clearly had ideas for herself that went beyond reality.

When he got started with Julie, he was actually pleased with the way she moved and listened to him. Even though she acted a little silly at times, she did what he told her to. By the time he was finished with her, he had more than a dozen shots that he promised to send her once they were developed.

Next came Ed. Nathan had always heard that Ed Phillips was one of the best-looking guys on campus, and he didn't doubt the man's charm with the ladies. But he wasn't the best subject for a photo shoot. He was awkward, and he hated being told what to do— the kiss of death for a model. Thank goodness he didn't have aspirations in that direction.

The moment he'd been dreading finally arrived. He crooked his finger toward Pamela and asked her to start out by the door. Her eyes were huge as she listened and tried to do what she thought he wanted her to do.

"Shouldn't we turn a fan on me so we can get some windblown-look pictures?" she asked.

She's been watching too many movies, he thought. "No, we're fine. Let's just work with what we've got."

Ed jumped up and ran toward the back room. "I'll get a fan."

Nathan gritted his teeth. This whole thing was so totally absurd he felt like he was in one of those dreams where nothing made a bit of sense.

Pamela clapped her hands together as Ed plugged in the fan and aimed it at her. She sat down on the ottoman and posed in the same position as a famous Marilyn Monroe photograph.

Nathan began to snap pictures while she turned from side to side, trying her best to look like a New York model. She sucked in her cheeks, she smiled with all her teeth showing, then she licked her lips and tried to take on a pouty look. None of it worked, but he kept right on taking pictures.

He managed several dozen before he finally called it quits. "What?" Pamela asked as she stood up and took his arm. "So soon? I was just beginning to have fun."

Ed narrowed his eyes and glared at Nathan. "Can't you take a few more?"

"No," Nathan said, shaking his head. "I don't think so. I have plenty for a beginner's portfolio."

Pamela looked up at him with adoring eyes and cooed, "When I get my first modeling job, I'm going to insist that you be my photographer, Nathan. I won't ever forget the people who helped me along the way."

Nathan had to stifle a chuckle. "I appreciate that, Miss Pritchett."

"Oh, please, call me Pamela. Miss Pritchett sounds so stuffy."

"Sorry," Nathan said. "Habit."

Ed had his arm slung over Julie's neck, and she looked like she was getting bored, but she went along with the program. "Hey, anyone up to a game of Twister?"

Nathan groaned. He hadn't played that silly game since junior high. "I don't think so, Ed. I've got to get up early in the morning and do a few things."

"Don't tell me you're calling it quits already?" Ed roared. "We're just now getting started."

Pamela looked puzzled. "But I thought—"

Nathan held his hands up and shook his head. "Why don't we have some coffee before I leave?"

Ed told the women to have a seat. On the way to the kitchen, he almost took Nathan's head off. "How dare you come here and get Pamela's hopes up, just to drop her like a bomb and leave?"

Nathan had heard enough. This was the final straw. "Look, Ed," he replied, glaring right back at his old friend. "I didn't want to be fixed up with anyone. I can get my own dates if I want them, and I don't want one right now. I took the pictures you asked me to take, and now I'm ready to leave."

Ed's face fell. Nathan would have felt sorry for the guy if he hadn't been so sneaky in what he was attempting. "Okay, Nathan. I just figured . . ." His voice trailed off as Nathan stood there staring at him.

"I know what you figured, and I'm not interested." Nathan tried to soften his own voice. "But thanks for thinking of me."

"Do you have someone in New York?"

"No, I really don't have time. My schedule is pretty tight when I'm working, which is most of the time. And I go on location a lot, which leaves very little time for a relationship."

"Do you think Pamela has much of a chance?" Ed asked, his voice a little shaky.

Nathan shrugged. Who was he to rain on someone's hope? "Never can tell about these things. Part of it is looks, part of it tenacity, but the majority is luck. You know, being in the right place at the right time."

"What should she do next?" Ed reached over and put coffee into the basket, then flipped the ON switch.

"I'll send her the developed glossies, and she can put them into a portfolio. She'll need to be ready to pound the pavement if she's really serious. That could take a very long time and a lot of hard work." Nathan left out the part about how many women did that and didn't succeed.

"Well, she's certainly pretty enough," Ed said.

Nathan couldn't bring himself to respond to that

comment. "I'll send everyone's pictures directly to you, and you can deliver them."

"Thanks, bud." Ed slapped Nathan on the back in a gesture he probably intended to make up for his earlier comment.

Nathan practically chugged his coffee so he could get out of there as fast as he could. Now that the picture-taking session was over, there really wasn't much to talk about.

Pamela and Julie both tried to find out information about the supermodels he came in contact with every day, but there wasn't much to say. He rarely saw them outside work, and he did his best to leave once they were finished. No one in his business had much time to socialize unless it was to further their career.

"Oh," Pamela said, disappointment evident on her face. "I was hoping for some fun tidbits of industry news."

"Well," Nathan said, digging deep in the back of his mind. "The major companies are starting to appreciate older models, since the population is aging as a group." He felt that he needed to give her something, no matter how lame it might be.

"I can do old," she said, standing up, hunching over, and contorting her face, making her look like she had gastrointestinal problems.

Nathan really had to get out of there. This was way too much to have to deal with.

It took him another half hour before he could leave

without a fight. When he got to the car, he let out a sigh of relief. At least he'd be back to his normal life in a few days. That was some consolation.

Nathan had to hold himself back so he wouldn't call Stephanie on Sunday. No sense spending more time with her and messing with his heart or his mind. He was afraid it would already be difficult to keep from thinking about her as it was.

First thing he did Monday morning was send a message to the classrooms of the people he was scheduled to take pictures of on Tuesday, requesting an earlier appointment. The male teacher agreed, but the female sent a message back saying she wasn't dressed for the occasion.

As soon as his last morning appointment was over on Monday, Nathan went straight to that teacher's classroom. She saw him standing at the door, and she motioned for him to wait just a moment. He watched as she gave instructions to her class, then reach for her brush. It was another couple of minutes before she met him in the hallway.

"I really don't want my picture taken today. This color is awful on me," she said, pointing to her blouse.

She was right.

"Tell you what," he said. "I have some fabric drapes I keep with my equipment. In fact, the green one would be perfect with your eyes."

Her whole face lit up.

"Green is my favorite color! Okay, then, I'll do it."

She backed up toward her classroom, her face glowing. "Are you sure?"

"Absolutely," he said, his heart lifting. He'd be able to go home tomorrow. He could even leave tonight if he got a flight out.

He left her and went outside to the back school yard to place the call on his cell phone. The airline reservation agent booked him on a flight out of there at midnight. What a relief.

Stephanie glanced outside the classroom window and did a double take. What was Nathan doing outside talking on the phone? It must have been very private and urgent based on the the look on his face.

She turned back around to the children working diligently on a math test. Now she wished she'd waited another day to give the test. She needed something to get her mind off Nathan, and teaching a lesson would be just the thing to do that.

Stephanie tried hard not to look out the window again. But the magnetic force of her attraction to Nathan kept pulling her attention over.

He was gone. *Thank goodness!* Now she could concentrate on answering questions when the children raised their hands during the test. The only problem was, no one had a single question.

The whole day dragged for Stephanie. She normally loved being in the classroom with her kids, but today was an exception.

She felt restless. She needed to get out of the school where she knew Nathan Holloway was still taking pictures.

During lunch she heard someone talking in the line ahead of her. When Nathan's name was mentioned, she strained to hear more.

"I heard he's been called back to New York to work on some big account."

"Yeah," another teacher said. "I heard it's for Revlon."

The first teacher shook her head. "I thought it was some blue jeans company."

Stephanie felt a pang of jealousy strike her heart. She had to turn the other way to keep anyone from noticing.

"Don't let it get to you, Steph," Marla said. Stephanie had almost forgotten who she was in line with.

"Don't let what get to me?" She had to pretend she didn't know what Marla was talking about.

"You know," Marla said, pointing to the chatty teachers ahead of them in line. "They don't know a thing. They're only speculating."

Stephanie shrugged. "It really doesn't matter, anyway. Nathan blew into town, and he's getting ready to blow out of town. That's the way it is with people like him."

"I don't think so, Steph," Marla replied. "I think he really cares for you."

Stephanie forced a chuckle. "He doesn't know me well enough to care."

"He knows enough. He's a smart man."

After a huge silence, Stephanie turned and looked her friend squarely in the eye. After all, what did she have to lose? "Men like Nathan don't take an interest in women like me. There are other, more glamorous women out there."

"You really don't know, do you?" Marla said, shaking her head in disbelief and rolling her eyes.

"I don't know what?"

"You're absolutely gorgeous, Steph. Maybe you went through an awkward stage as a teenager, but you've pulled out of it. No one in this town holds a candle to you. You're way out of everyone else's league in the classy department."

"Oh, come on, Marla," Stephanie said as her face grew warm with embarrassment.

"It's true. And Nathan noticed it."

"He did not." *No way,* she thought.

"He came over and talked with Hank and me one night after school."

"He did?" Stephanie squeaked. "Nathan Holloway?"

Marla nodded. "And I'll give you one guess what we talked about."

"I have no idea."

"Oh, I think you do," Marla said. "But I'll play your game. He wanted to discuss you."

"Me?"

"Yes, you. And Mr. Phillips and Pamela and the whole crazy town."

Naturally, he'd want to discuss Pamela. Didn't everyone? "I hope you didn't say anything too bad about anyone."

Marla tossed her hair back and laughed. "Sweet Stephanie, always doing the right thing." Then she grew quiet as she looked directly at Stephanie and softly said, "I didn't say anything I shouldn't have said."

Stephanie shrugged. "But nothing has changed, has it? We're still here in Hartsville, Mr. Phillips is still the principal and our boss, and Miss Pritchett is still the reigning queen of the town."

"That's the last thing you need to think about," Marla said. "I think you should go speak to Nathan before he leaves. And I have a hunch he's leaving before he originally planned to."

"Obviously," Stephanie agreed. A person would have had to be deaf to not hear the conversation in the lunch line. She thought about it for a moment, then began to back away from the line. "I'm really not all that hungry, Marla. Go ahead and eat without me."

"Tell Nathan I said it was really nice getting to know him."

"Okay," Stephanie answered as she turned and walked as fast as she could to the classroom where Nathan was set up. Hopefully, he'd still be there.

Yes, he was. And he wasn't alone, either. Mr. Phillips was in there trying to talk him out of leaving so soon. She paused by the door.

Right when she looked inside, Nathan glanced up and smiled. Not just a slight grin, either. She was the recipient of a great big, sincere, toothy smile. Her heart pounded so hard it almost jumped out of her mouth.

Mr. Phillips turned around to see what Nathan was grinning about. He took one look at her, flicked his hand up to stop her, then turned back to Nathan.

Nathan frowned. "Wait a minute, Ed. Don't tell Stephanie to stop." He motioned for her to come on in.

Stephanie didn't know what to do. Ed Phillips was her boss. The last thing she needed to do was disobey him.

Mr. Phillips noticed her hesitation, and a tiny grin tweaked the corners of his lips. He liked the fact that she respected his position, and she could tell he was about to take advantage of it.

Something came over her right then that she never knew she had in her. She boldly entered the room, crossed over to where Mr. Phillips and Nathan were standing, and sauntered right up beside them. Mr.

Phillips's grin left his face, turning red with what she thought might be rage.

"I'm glad you dropped by, Steph," Nathan said as he reached out for her. "I'm leaving tonight, and I wanted to say good-bye."

"So I heard," she said cautiously, not knowing how to handle Mr. Phillips's presence. "I just wanted to thank you for being so kind as to come here and help us with our first yearbook."

Nathan chuckled. "I didn't exactly have a choice. This man really holds the power of persuasion."

Mr. Phillips cautiously glanced back and forth between Nathan and Stephanie. "I'll go talk to Miss Pritchett and have her come right down," he said. "I'm sure she'll want to offer her gratitude as well."

As soon as he left the room, Nathan let out a soft snicker. "He's really trying too hard, you know."

Stephanie nodded. "Yes, I know. But he means well."

"He's a fool."

"A what?" She thought they were friends.

"Yeah, he's a fool. He's so in love with Pamela Pritchett he doesn't know what to do."

"Mr. Phillips is in love with Pamela? I don't think so."

"Just watch them for a moment when they come in here," he said.

Within seconds, Pamela and Mr. Phillips were headed through the classroom door, she in the lead and he right behind. Stephanie studied them for signs of anything other than a working relationship.

As soon as Mr. Phillips led Pamela toward Nathan, she saw a few things she hadn't noticed before. Like the way his hand went to the small of her back as he gently guided her toward and Nathan. And the way his eyes looked down at her with total adoration.

Nathan was right!

She quickly glanced over at Nathan, and he actually winked. Right in front of her boss and Pamela! And she knew they saw it, too.

Pamela, not one to be outdone, pulled away from Mr. Phillips and threw her arms around Nathan's neck, giving him a huge hug. Nathan just stood there like a stick, looking extremely uncomfortable.

"I wish you didn't have to leave so soon, Nathan, honey," she cooed. "And we were just getting to know each other."

Stephanie instantly felt sick. She cast a nervous glance over at Mr. Phillips, and he stood very still, almost like he was afraid to move. Pamela remained hanging on Nathan, who wasn't moving, either. If she didn't have such bad feelings toward Pamela, it would have been funny.

Finally, after what seemed like forever, Nathan reached down and peeled Pamela off himself and gently shoved her toward Mr. Phillips, who reached out and eased her close to his chest. Then he let go.

Pamela looked like a scared rabbit as she glanced

back and forth between both men, not sure which one she needed to please. Stephanie just stared. This was all too weird for her.

One thing she did know for certain was that Nathan was absolutely right about Mr. Phillips's feelings toward Pamela. Why hadn't she seen it before? Was she blind to the obvious? Apparently so.

"I've had such a wonderful time here in Hartsville," Nathan said, looking at Stephanie the whole time. "You were right, Ed," he added, turning toward his friend. "Hartsville really does have the most beautiful women in the world."

Mr. Phillips smiled at Pamela with pride. "Yes, we do, don't we? And the prettiest one of all teaches right here at my school."

Stephanie couldn't believe what her eyes actually saw. Pamela Pritchett blushed! This was a first.

"Why, thank you, Eddie," she said, forgetting they were in the company of another teacher. "I mean, Mr. Phillips."

Pamela glanced down at her shoes then back up at Nathan, more subdued this time. "I hope you decide to come back sometime, Nathan. It was such a pleasure to meet you."

"Pleasure's all mine," he replied.

"And you will get to my pictures right away and let me know if anyone's interested, won't you?" she asked with the eagerness of a little girl.

"I'll develop the pictures and send them to you,

but I'm afraid you'll have to generate interest on your own," Nathan said apologetically.

Mr. Phillips reached out and touched Pamela reassuringly. "I'll help you."

Again, she blushed. Those two were so in love they were silly. And the most amazing thing about it was that neither of them realized it.

"Well, I'd better get back to my work," Nathan said. "I don't want to slight anyone just because I have to leave."

Stephanie smiled at him with shaky lips. "Thanks again, Nathan. I hope things keep going well for you in New York."

Her heart ached as she left the room, knowing that her chances of ever seeing this man again were close to nil. As much as she hated to admit it, she was more than just attracted to him. There was much more. There was already an emotional bond, and they'd only been around each other a few times.

That afternoon, teaching her squirmy class was the most difficult thing she'd ever done. She could hardly wait to get out of there and to her little house where her heart was safe.

As Stephanie left the makeshift studio, Nathan felt like a huge chunk of his heart was walking out the door. He'd grown to feel something for that woman, and he knew that she would never make the effort to see him again. At least, he didn't think she would.

Stephanie Mansfield had some convoluted notion that she belonged in this town. He didn't think so. They didn't appreciate what a wonderful and beautiful woman she'd grown into.

But what did it matter to him now? He'd be leaving tonight, and she chose to remain in this place.

She's a grown woman, he told himself over and over. She could do anything she pleased, and if that meant hanging around where she wasn't appreciated, then what did it matter to him?

As the rest of his appointments came to have their pictures taken, he noticed their expressions of concern when he greeted them with a growl. They shouldn't have worried. He never let his mood affect his work. He was a professional. He was Nathan Holloway.

The second his last person left, Nathan packed up his camera equipment and made a beeline for the door. He was almost to his rental car when Marla and her husband Hank skidded to a stop in the parking lot beside him. Where had they come from?

"Hi, Nathan," Marla called out the window. "We just wanted to tell you how much we enjoyed meeting you."

Nathan offered a closed-mouth grin and a mock salute. "Nice meeting you, too."

Hank spoke up. "If you'd ever like to come back to Hartsville, you can stay with us. You don't have to go to a hotel."

"Thanks," Nathan said as he loaded is equipment. He had no intention of returning to Hartsville, so what use was it to tell them he preferred a hotel? "I'll be sure to call you if I ever come back."

Marla got out of the car, slammed the door, and leaned against it with her arms folded across her chest. She stood there and glared at him.

"What?" he said after he couldn't take the discomfort of having her look at him like that anymore.

"You're never coming back, are you?" she said matter-of-factly.

"Don't plan to," he replied, working hard at keeping the growl from his voice.

"Oh, that's just fine, Nathan," she ranted, waving her arms around like a madwoman as she pulled away from the car. "Go ahead. Just run away. Leave. Never mind the fact that you and Stephanie Mansfield might have a good thing going on."

"What?" he repeated. "Did I do something wrong?"

"Oh, no," she answered with sarcasm. "Not unless you consider denying your true feelings to be doing something wrong."

Nathan shook his head and managed a snicker. But he didn't feel like laughing. He knew something wasn't right about leaving now, but he couldn't hang around. There were things to do and contacts to make in the city.

"Nathan," she said, her voice dragging out the last

syllable of his name. "You're gonna regret it if you just take off like this."

"That's the risk I'll have to take," he said half-heartedly.

She threw her hands up and got back in the car. "I give up. Some people can be so hardheaded. You and Stephanie were made for each other, and I can't seem to get through to either one of you."

That got Nathan's attention. He turned and spoke directly to Marla. "You spoke to Stephanie?"

"Of course I did. You don't expect me to mind my own business, do you?"

"I guess not." He swallowed hard. "What did she say?"

"Basically, the same thing you're saying. Except she told me that if you wanted her to come to the airport to see you off, you'd call her and ask her to. But I told her that was ridiculous."

"She'd do that?"

"What?" Marla asked, rolling her eyes.

"She'd come to see me off at the airport?"

"I don't know, Nathan," she replied as she began to roll up her window. "Why don't you ask her yourself?"

Nathan slammed his hands against his car. He had fully intended to pick up his things at the hotel, pack the rental car, and drive straight to the airport where he'd have dinner while waiting for his flight. Now he had other ideas, and that bothered him.

The very thought of seeing Stephanie again made him happy. He really enjoyed being around her. She soothed his soul, and she made him feel more important than just a world-famous photographer. He felt like a real man.

What harm would there be in asking her to have dinner with him before he left? That might be fun.

Chapter Nine

"Y̶ou want me to see you off at the airport?" Stephanie asked. Why had he called her right when she was working so hard at forgetting he even existed?

"Sure," he replied. "That is, if you'd like to have dinner with me."

Stephanie let out a huge sigh. There was no way she could turn him down. She wanted to see Nathan more than she even wanted to take her next breath.

Should she? Probably not.

But would she?

"Yes, Nathan," she replied. "I'd love to."

"Good," he said quickly. "Since I have a rental car that needs to be returned, I have to ask you to drive yourself to the airport. That is, if you don't mind."

"N-no, of course, I don't mind." Stephanie drove

all over the place by herself. Why would that bother her?

"How's seven?" he asked.

"Seven's fine."

He told her where to meet him, and then they hung up. Stephanie just stood there in front of the big picture window and stared at the sky that Nathan had been so enthralled with. It really was beautiful with all the blues and pinks merging and swirling in lines above the trees.

Stephanie didn't take too long getting ready since she knew it would take her at least a half hour to drive to the airport. Hartsville was too small to have its own airport, so she had to go all the way to Baker, which was twenty miles away.

All the way there, Stephanie told herself over and over that she and Nathan were just pals. Buddies. Someone to talk to.

But deep in her heart she knew better. She really liked him. In fact, if given half a chance she knew she would probably fall in love with him. No other man had ever made her feel so alive, so beautiful, and so special.

The drive there was long, but the weather was perfect. As the sun began to set behind the trees, Stephanie remembered the times she'd spent with Nathan and how much she appreciated everything about nature. He had a way of bringing out the best in everything.

She found a spot in short-term parking pretty quickly. Nathan was waiting for her right where he told her he'd be. The instant their gazes met, his eyes crinkled, and a smile broke out on his lips. Her heart melted.

Nathan guided her into the restaurant where the hostess seated them. "I hope you like seafood," he said. "I've heard it's their specialty."

"I like anything," Stephanie admitted. "It's a wonder I'm not as big as a house."

He laughed out loud. "I like a woman who's not afraid to eat."

"I suppose you're used to being around models who eat like birds, huh?"

Nathan nodded, studying her face intently, which should have made her feel uncomfortable. But she didn't. She just looked back at him in wonder and amazement that anyone would find her so interesting.

"Well, I'm the first to admit, I'm a big eater. But at least I get plenty of exercise on my property."

"What do you do?" he asked.

Stephanie shrugged as she thought about everything she'd done all her life with her grandmother and now had to do alone. "I mow the lawn, weed the flower beds, mulch, trim, and in the springtime, I plant flowers."

"Sounds wonderful," he said. "I have to go to the gym to work out."

Stephanie felt warm as his gaze continued to linger

on her. Nathan had a way of making her feel as though she was the only woman on earth worth paying attention to.

The meal was delicious, and time flew by. Before she was ready for him to leave, Nathan's flight was called over the public address system.

She walked him to his boarding gate and just stood there while he rearranged his camera case. "Stephanie," he whispered softly.

Stephanie had the strange feeling that he was about to kiss her. Why now? Couldn't he have left her alone, untouched? But she couldn't resist.

As his arms went around her waist, Stephanie felt herself melting against him. Their lips came together briefly, then he pulled away, his face flushed.

"I really need to go now," he said huskily.

She licked her lips and nodded. " 'Bye, Nathan. And thanks for everything."

As he walked away from her, Stephanie's heart ached. She wanted to run after him, to tell him to wait for her to pack her bags so she could join him. But she didn't. It wasn't the right thing to do. He lived in New York where he did his photographing, and she was a teacher at Hartsville Elementary School. Their lives were very different.

Now that he was gone, Stephanie wished she had never met Nathan Holloway. All she had left were memories. Memories and a sweet taste on her lips from his kiss. And she wanted more.

* * *

It was time to get back to the hustle and bustle of city life, Nathan thought as he watched out the window while the plane taxied down the runway. Back to endless photo shoots and models with sharp cheekbones and attitudes to match.

All he had left to do for the people of Hartsville was develop their pictures and send them back for their brand-new yearbook. Why Ed Phillips had requested he come, Nathan would never figure out. Anyone could have done what he did.

The flight back was uneventful. Since it was a short flight, only a snack was served, which was fine. Nathan was still full from dinner. He just ordered a soft drink and peanuts.

The second he reached his apartment, he opened the door, tossed his luggage in his bedroom, and went to the answering machine to check his messages. The only messages were from agents and his studio.

Disappointment flowed through him, but he didn't know why. Who did he expect to call? Surely not anyone else. He wasn't dating anyone, and the few friends he had in New York knew he was out of town.

It was 3:00 in the morning, but he wasn't sleepy. After unpacking his things and putting his camera equipment away, he headed for the living room and picked up the remote control to do a little channel surfing. Nothing good on television, but what did he expect? Not exactly prime time.

Finally, shortly after the sun began to lighten the sky, Nathan began to feel his eyelids droop. He knew better than to fight it. He could sleep until noon if he wanted to, since he didn't have any appointments. His original plans were to return today, anyway, so he'd just take the day to rest.

Unfortunately, he'd forgotten to turn off the ringer on the phone. It woke him at 10:00.

"Nathan," one of the modeling agents said the second he answered. "I'm glad you're back. We've got people screaming at us from all sides to get this photo work done."

He let out a sigh as he rubbed his aching neck. That awful pain had returned. "What do you want me to do?"

"Since I know you're booked tomorrow, can you squeeze a shoot in at Central Park this afternoon?"

"I suppose I could. What time?" This was the last thing he wanted. Or needed. Rest was more on his mind than ever. Nathan hadn't realized until now how weary he was from that trip to Hartsville.

"Two o'clock," she replied. "But it shouldn't take more than a couple of hours."

Nathan knew better. A couple of hours could easily turn into five or six long, tedious hours of picture after picture, until he managed to get enough to have something decent.

"I'll be there. Just do me a favor and call my office to get the rest of my equipment."

"I'll do that," she said, with gratitude evident in her voice.

One of the reasons Nathan had been so successful in this big city was because he was willing to stick his neck out and go the extra mile. And he rarely turned down a job, no matter how exhausted he was.

The photo shoot went amazingly well. It only took four hours. "Thanks for doing such a good job," he told the model, a woman he'd worked with before and enjoyed photographing. She was one of those rare ones who didn't have to look in a mirror every few minutes.

"Nathan, you seem different somehow," she said.

"What?" He was taken aback by her strange, out-of-the-blue comment.

"I don't know," she said, shrugging. "You seem different. Softer maybe. You remind me of my brother when he first fell in love with his wife." She tilted her head to one side and asked, "Did you meet someone?"

"I'm always meeting new people," he growled back.

She giggled. "Don't try to play macho with me, Nathan. It's not working. I have a brother, remember?"

"Yeah, that's right." He chuckled as he reached out and squeezed her shoulder in a gentle, brotherly way. "Yes, I did meet someone."

"Someone special?" she asked with delight.

Nathan nodded. "But unfortunately, she's several hundred miles away."

"That's what jets are for," she said with understanding.

"No good." He began to pack his equipment for what seemed like the hundredth time that day. "But thanks for asking."

"Nathan," she said before she left, "don't let your work get in the way of your heart. I'd hate to see you grow old all alone, just because you can't figure out how to make this work. You're a creative man. Do something."

He looked at her for a moment before casting his glance downward. "See you later, okay?"

"I can take a hint," she said as she backed away. "Have a good day, Nathan."

The second she was out of sight, Nathan put down the stand he'd been working on. That world-class model knew something about life that he needed to learn. And he was determined to find out what it was.

Where should he start?

He was here in New York, while the woman he wanted to be with was in Hartsville. He couldn't go back there. Not now, anyway.

She had a regular, full-time job that she loved. And a house. Not an easy obstacle to overcome.

Perhaps a phone call would help. Yeah, that's what he'd do. He'd call her and listen to her voice. Maybe that would make him feel better.

Nathan could hardly wait to finish packing his things so he could get back to his apartment and call Stephanie. He managed to do it in record time.

He raced for the door, unlocked it, dropped his gear, and grabbed the phone like a lovesick man. Then he realized he didn't know her number.

It took him several minutes to locate it, but the second he got it, he punched the numbers out on the phone pad. She answered on the second ring. She was home!

"Stephanie," he said as calmly as he could. "This is Nathan."

"Nathan?" she said, sounding like she wasn't sure she believed him. "Where are you?"

"New York." Man, it was great to hear her voice. She sounded like an angel.

"I'm glad you made it back safely," she said slowly.

Nathan sank down on the chair and luxuriated in the comfort of talking to Stephanie Mansfield. She elicited feelings from him that he wasn't even aware existed. But it was like looking at candy from the other side of the glass counter. He could look and crave, but he couldn't taste its sweetness. He had to see her again.

"I want you to come to New York, Steph," he said boldly and out of the blue.

"You what?" she said disbelievingly.

"You heard me," he replied. "When do you get a long weekend?"

"Well," she said slowly enough to drive him crazy, "I have a Monday off in two weeks."

"Then I'll fly you here on Friday, and you can return on Monday."

"But how?" she asked with a giggle.

"Don't worry about a thing," he replied. "I'll send the tickets, and you can stay with Rhonda."

"Who's Rhonda?"

"Rhonda Ladnier," he replied.

"Supermodel Rhonda Ladnier?"

"Yes, that's the one."

"B-but Nathan, I don't know her," she stuttered.

"You'll love her, Steph. Trust me. Besides, it was her idea for you to come, anyway."

"It was?" Her voice sounded small and squeaky. Nathan loved surprising her like this.

As soon as they got off the phone, he dialed Rhonda's number. "You were right," he said as soon as she picked up the phone. "Oh, this is Nathan, by the way."

"I knew that," she said with a husky chuckle. "And I'm always right. But what about this time?"

"I decided to call the woman I want to be with, and she's coming in two weeks."

"Good, Nathan."

"And she's staying with you."

"Uh, Nathan, are you asking me, or do I have a choice?"

"I've already told her she could," he pleaded. "I hope that's okay."

There was a brief pause, but she finally said, "That'll be fine. But next time talk to me first."

"I thought I already did."

"You're too much, Nathan."

"And I expect you to tell her all the wonderful things about me."

"Oh, I'll tell her all about you, all right. Just wait."

Nathan felt like singing. And he did. He hopped into the shower and sang at the top of his lungs. Stephanie was coming to see him, and he was going to have the time of his life.

What had just happened? Stephanie hung up the phone and stared at her grandmother's picture for a few seconds before she sucked in a deep breath. Had Nathan just called and asked her to visit him in New York for the weekend?

That was something New Yorkers did. Not people from Hartsville. Stephanie was used to going for long Sunday drives, having picnics at the park, and going to the movies with friends. But a weekend trip to New York?

First thing she did when she came to her senses was dial Marla's number. Stephanie told her what she'd agreed to do.

"That's fantastic!" Marla exclaimed.

"But he said I can stay with Rhonda Ladnier."

"Ooh, she's so bee-eau-ti-ful," Marla said, drawing out the word and making extra syllables.

"Yes, she is, but I gather she and Nathan are very good friends."

"To have friends like that, who needs enemies?"

Stephanie had no idea what Marla meant by that, but she didn't care. She needed advice. "What do I do, Marla?"

"What do you mean, what do you do? You go and you have a good time."

"How can I? I've never been to New York."

"That's precisely my point, Steph. I'll help you shop, and then Hank and I will take you to Baker and see you off at the airport."

"I don't know . . ." Stephanie began. Although she wanted to see Nathan even more than she realized before, she was still unsure of whether or not it was a good idea.

"Don't be ridiculous," Marla said. She was relentless. There was no arguing with her.

The two weeks went by in a daze for Stephanie.

Next thing she knew she was packing her bags, filling them with the brand-new outfits Marla had helped her pick out for the trip. "People in New York are very fashion-conscious, you know. I don't want you to stick out like a sore thumb."

At the airport, Hank shook her hand, and Marla hugged her for a long time. "Don't let this opportunity get away, Steph. You and Nathan are meant for each other."

"How do you know that?" Stephanie asked.

"I just feel it."

That was good enough for Marla, but Stephanie didn't know if she should pay much attention to her friend's feelings. Feelings got you into trouble. She'd always been more analytical and weighed things out.

But was she happy? Well, she wasn't unhappy. However, she knew something was missing in her life.

The flight to New York was uneventful. She stepped out of the connecting tunnel and looked around for Nathan. At first she didn't see him, but once she reached the terminal, she felt familiar arms reach out and embrace her.

It was Nathan. Her heart nearly stopped, so that when it began to pound, she could hear it in her ears. Nothing could compare to the feeling she had when she was with him. Maybe Marla was right.

"Tired?" he asked as he took her bag.

"Not really," she answered. She was too excited.

"Good. I'll take you to Rhonda's place and introduce you to your weekend roommate, then we'll go
out for a little while. New York nightlife never ends,
you know."

Stephanie still couldn't believe all this. First of all,
she'd impulsively traveled to New York, a place
she'd never been to in her life. And she was staying
with someone she'd only seen in magazines and on
television commercials. It seemed so unreal.

They were met at the door by a woman wearing
bike pants and a loose T-shirt, definitely not the most
stylish outfit Stephanie had seen in her life, even in
Hartsville. She took in the whole effect of the person,
which seemed pretty normal, until she looked into
the woman's eyes. There was a sparkle there that
truly made her seem special. Bigger than life. It was
almost magical.

"Hi, Stephanie," she said as she helped bring the
bags into her apartment. "Nathan has told me so
much about you, I feel like I already know you." She
led the way to a bedroom toward the back of the
apartment. "I'm Rhonda Ladnier," she said once she
put Stephanie's things down. "And if you need anything let me know."

Stephanie took her extended hand and just stared,
smiling, not knowing quite what to say. She cleared
her throat and managed a squeaky, "Nice to meet
you, Rhonda."

Neither Rhonda nor Nathan seemed to notice her

intimidation by this supermodel who looked anything but stylish right now. But regardless of what she wore, she still looked beautiful.

After Stephanie had all her things in the room, Rhonda nudged the two of them out the door and handed Stephanie a key. "You two go on and have a good time. I'll probably be asleep when you get back, so you'll have to let yourself in."

As soon as Stephanie and Nathan were outside, she turned to him and said, "She goes to bed this early?"

He nodded. "Yes, models have to be rested before they have a full day of photo shoots. They can't afford to have puffy eyes."

"She works on Saturdays?"

"In spite of what people seem to think, the life of a model isn't all that glamorous. And it isn't easy, either."

"I didn't realize what they had to sacrifice," Stephanie said.

"Would you like to go watch Rhonda's session for a few minutes tomorrow?" Nathan asked.

"Sure," Stephanie replied. "That is, if you don't mind."

"No, I was hoping *you* wouldn't mind since I wanted to check up on the photographer I threw this job to. When you agreed to come, I told Rhonda I couldn't do the photos."

"You gave up work for me?" she asked. Stephanie wasn't sure if she should feel flattered or if she should apologize for messing up his schedule. But then she remembered he was the one who'd asked her to come.

"Yes, I did," he replied in a soft, husky voice. The look he gave her melted her all the way to her toes.

Stephanie accepted Nathan's hand as he offered it. They walked down the street that was as busy as Main Street in Hartsville during rush hour. Everyone seemed focused on something ahead of them.

"Well," Nathan began, "what do you think of New York so far?"

"It—it's all so amazingly big," she replied, looking up at one of the hundreds of skyscrapers.

"Yes, it is," he said with a chuckle.

"Where are we going?"

Nathan squeezed her shoulders and whispered in her ear, "You'll see in just a few minutes."

Chapter Ten

Nathan led her a few more blocks, and they went inside one of the buildings she would have missed if he hadn't been with her. She still had no idea what he was up to until they came to a door with the name "Jenko's Comedy Club" in neon letters above it.

That sounded like a lot of fun to Stephanie. She loved to laugh, and it seemed that she didn't do nearly enough of it anymore.

He ordered for both of them, and they just sat there and waited for the first act. "Rhonda suggested I bring you here," he explained. "She told me that was one of the things she enjoyed most about living in New York."

"Where's she from?" Stephanie asked. Rhonda had

seemed like such a sweet person, unlike what she'd imagined a supermodel to be like.

"A small town similar to Hartsville. Somewhere in the Midwest."

Stephanie really enjoyed watching one standup comedian after another. She couldn't remember ever laughing so hard in her life.

They got back to Rhonda's apartment shortly after midnight. She let herself in with the key and tiptoed to her room to keep from waking up her hostess. It was very generous for Rhonda to have offered her a place to stay.

The next morning, she awoke bright and early, even though she hadn't gotten much sleep. She was too excited. This was New York, and she didn't want to miss a moment of action.

"What are you doing up so early?" Rhonda asked from the hallway. She stood there in a jogging suit, her hair piled up on top of her head in a big clip. "I hope I didn't wake you."

"No," Stephanie said, amazed at how naturally beautiful this person was. "Nathan said we could watch your photo shoot for a little while this morning."

Rhonda grinned mischievously. "He's checking up on his replacement. Sly dog."

It was so easy to talk with Rhonda, Stephanie nearly forgot who she was. "Can you blame him?"

"Not really," Rhonda replied. "Nathan's the best photographer in New York."

Stephanie felt warm all over, hearing that, but she tried her best to conceal her pride in the man with whom she was quickly falling in love. But Rhonda studied her with a knowing look in her eyes.

"Well, gotta run now. See you later in the park." Rhonda left with a bag slung over one shoulder and her hair flopping around over the clip. *It must be nice to look so good this early in the morning,* Stephanie thought.

She walked down the street to a deli she'd seen the night before and picked up a few items to share with Rhonda. She didn't want to wear out her welcome.

Nathan called an hour after she got back to Rhonda's apartment. "Rested?"

"I feel great!"

"Well, good, then, are you ready?" he asked.

"I will be by the time you get here."

He was there in fifteen minutes. It felt totally natural to walk down the streets of New York City with Nathan. People scurried around in all directions. Stephanie couldn't remember ever feeling so wonderful in her entire life.

The photo shoot was different from anything she'd ever seen. It was definitely a change from being a teacher in Hartsville. She thoroughly enjoyed watching how Rhonda worked. Nathan even told her that she'd be able to see the results in the next season's magazines. That excited her.

Everything about New York was alive and full of an energy that Stephanie couldn't describe. But she also knew it wasn't her life. It was almost like she was living in someone else's skin while she was here.

The long weekend ended much too soon to suit her, but when it was time to go, she was ready. Nathan stood by the departure gate and held her in his arms.

"I had a wonderful time, Nathan," she said in all honesty.

"Me, too." Nathan rested his chin on her head and just held her.

"When can you come back to Hartsville?" Stephanie pulled away to see the expression on his face.

He shook his head. "I'd like to come in a few weeks, but just for a weekend. I'll have to be discreet, though, because I'm only coming to see you."

That simple and direct comment made Stephanie tingle with excitement and pleasure all over. He obviously enjoyed being with her, or he wouldn't be going to so much trouble.

"That sounds good."

"Yeah," he added. "Marla and Hank told me that I could stay with them."

"They did?" This was the first she'd ever heard of that.

"Yes, and I plan to take them up on it more than

once, too. If I stay in a hotel, Ed will find out I'm in town, and he might try matchmaking again."

"I don't know why he doesn't just ask Pamela out himself," Stephanie said.

Nathan laughed out loud, his head tilted back. "Is Ed the only one who doesn't realize how in love with her he is?"

"Evidently."

"Someone needs to talk some sense into that guy."

The final boarding call came, and Stephanie had to leave. She felt torn, since she didn't like the idea of leaving Nathan. However, she did need to get back.

Over the next six months, Stephanie and Nathan took turns visiting each other. Each time they went their separate ways, Nathan felt it increasingly difficult to be without her. By now he knew he was in love with the woman, and there was no way out. He couldn't get enough of her.

But he had his work in New York. Nathan knew he couldn't make a living as a photographer in Hartsville. And Stephanie still felt attached to her property, and he couldn't blame her. It was a wonderful place. He even had to admit he'd thought about what a great place it would be to raise children.

Stephanie was due to arrive in a few days, and he'd been feeling pretty blue. She and Rhonda had become very good friends, and Stephanie had shared her feelings with the model.

When Rhonda told Nathan she couldn't betray a friend and tell a secret, he knew they'd discussed some of the things he'd been thinking about. "But I can tell you one thing, Nathan. Steph really cares for you quite a lot."

He shook his head. "But it seems hopeless to keep going like we are."

She grinned back at him and replied, "When you're in love, nothing's hopeless. You'll find a solution."

"I certainly hope so. My heart can't take much more of this."

"Then you're motivated to work hard on your solution," Rhonda said, that big, dopey grin still on her face.

He wished he had as much confidence as Rhonda that he'd figure out what to do. Every day without Stephanie was pure torture.

From the moment he picked her up to the time he dropped her off at the departure gate, Nathan acted funny all weekend. Stephanie couldn't for the life of her figure out what she'd said or done to make him be like this.

She asked him, and all he'd said was, "Nothing," in a quick grunt.

All the way home, on the flight, Stephanie racked her brain for an answer, but she couldn't come up with one. Maybe he was getting tired of her.

Stephanie got home and unpacked her bags, thinking she'd just go to bed early. Maybe tomorrow she'd feel better.

But the phone rang. It was Marla. "Well, how'd it go?"

"Not so good," Stephanie told her friend. "I think Nathan's getting tired of our long-distance relationship."

"I'm sure he is."

"I guess that means it's over, then." Stephanie's knees buckled beneath her, and she sank down on the edge of the bed. She loved Nathan, and breaking off the relationship was like cutting off her air. But it was inevitable, sooner or later. People who lived that far apart couldn't keep this up.

"Don't be so sure of that, Steph," Marla said.

"Oh, but I am."

Sure enough, the entire week went by, and Nathan didn't call. That was unusual. Over the past few months, he'd called her every night, with the exception of those times when he had to work late.

"I don't understand it," Marla said. "He and Hank had a long talk last time he was here, and Hank seemed to think . . ." Her voice trailed off, and a tiny smile flickered on her lips.

"What?" Stephanie said as she nudged her friend.

"Oh, nothing."

Stephanie rolled her eyes and let out an exasperated sigh. Marla was playing one of her games again. Well, Stephanie didn't have the energy to try to pull anything out of her right now. She was too depressed about Nathan's lack of attention.

Then, on the following Monday, Mr. Phillips called her into his office. She went there, thinking it had something to do with her class.

"Sit down," Mr. Phillips said, pointing to a chair across the desk from where he sat.

She did as she was told. "Is something wrong?"

"No," he said. Then, he narrowed his eyes and corrected himself. "Yes."

All her blood rushed to her feet. What had happened? It must have been pretty bad for Mr. Phillips to call her down to the office in the middle of the day like this.

"I understand you and Nathan Holloway have been seeing each other," he continued, still glaring at her.

What should she say? She couldn't lie to her boss, but she didn't want to divulge Nathan's secret—that he'd come to Hartsville without letting his old friend know. It was bound to come out sooner or later.

"Well, yes," she said as she folded her arms across her chest. She suddenly felt defenseless.

He nodded. "Yeah, that's what Nathan said when he called me last night."

"He called you?" Stephanie forgot all about being

the proper little teacher suddenly, and she sat forward, wanting to hear more.

"Yes, he called me, and he told me that he was thinking about moving to Hartsville."

"He did?"

"I don't know how you did it, Miss Mansfield. I've been trying to get him here for years, and the only way I could even get him to visit was to get him to do the pictures of the staff for the yearbook. He owed me a favor, and he's an honorable man."

"I-I'm sure it has nothing to do with me," Stephanie said. Her ears were ringing, and her mouth went dry. This was such a surprise.

"Well, I'm sure it has *everything* to do with you, Miss Mansfield. In fact, Nathan told me it does. That guy's so in love with you, he doesn't know if he's coming or going."

Stephanie felt like jumping up and grabbing her boss and giving him a big bear hug. But she didn't. She just sat there and let his words sink in. Nathan was in love with her? Why hadn't he told her? Mr. Phillips must be mistaken. But no, evidently Nathan had told him so. Still, it seemed too good to be true.

"You may go back to your class now, Miss Mansfield."

Stephanie stood up on wobbly legs, and somehow she managed to make it back to her classroom. She gave the kids an easy assignment to get them through the rest of the day, and right before they left to go home, she made the announcement, "No homework tonight. Play outside, watch TV, do whatever you want to do. But come tomorrow ready to work."

The kids all looked at one another and broke into a cheer. Stephanie was in such a good mood, she cheered right along with them.

As soon as Stephanie got to her car when it was time to go home, she just sat there. What if Mr. Phillips was mistaken? Wouldn't Nathan have said something to her if he'd planned to move to Hartsville? Surely he would.

The only way she could find out for certain was to ask him. She turned her key in the ignition and headed home as fast as she dared drive. She needed to find out.

Stephanie ran inside her little house, dropped her things on the floor, grabbed the phone, and punched out Nathan's number. She knew it by heart now. It rang four times before the answering machine picked up.

She opened her mouth to leave a message, but she couldn't. Nathan hadn't called her in quite some time, and she was confused. She licked her lips and carefully dropped the phone back down on the receiver.

How could she find out if Nathan was getting ready to move to Hartsville for sure? She supposed she could call Mr. Phillips and find out more from him, but she didn't want to do that.

Or she could call a friend who worked in the only real estate office in town. Hartsville was such a small place, not much got by that office. No, she didn't need to start nosing around and alarming people about what she'd heard.

The only thing Stephanie could think to do was sit back and wait. Wait for Nathan to contact her. That sounded like total torture to Stephanie.

But what choice did she have? Stephanie felt like her thoughts were becoming repetitive, although she couldn't help herself. Ever since she'd begun to care about Nathan, she had too many disturbing thoughts. When she was with him, she worried whether he was having fun with her. When she was away from him, she worried about what he was doing and if he was thinking about her as much as she thought about him. Then this past week held a different kind of worry for her. Since he hadn't called she naturally assumed he'd totally lost interest and moved onto something else.

Nathan's photography meant everything to him; it was his life's passion. He did it as a vocation and a hobby, always taking his camera whenever he went someplace. And she didn't mind, something he said he appreciated about her.

Stephanie went back through the house and started picking up all her things she'd dropped. It was stupid to let a man get to her like this. When she saw other women putting their lives on hold for guys, she thought they were weak and dependent. That's not the way she wanted to act.

Okay, Stephanie, she told herself. *Get a grip. There is life after being in love. It'll be hard, but you've got to do it.*

Right when she had everything picked up and put away, the phone rang. Stephanie jumped.

Calm down. It's probably just Marla.

Chapter Eleven

"Steph?"

It was Nathan! Stephanie's heart raced. She opened her mouth, but nothing came out.

"Steph, are you there?"

She cleared her throat and squeaked, "Yes. I'm here."

"Stephanie, we need to talk," he blurted out in one breath.

She thought she might faint. "We do?"

"Yes. Are you going to be home this weekend?"

"I'm not going anywhere, Nathan," she managed to say in spite of the lump in her throat.

"I'm coming there, and I don't care who you tell. We need to talk," he repeated. "This can't wait."

Stephanie gulped. He needed to talk to her? She wasn't sure if that was good.

"Okay, Nathan," she said softly. "I'll be here. Do you want me to tell Marla you're coming?"

"No," he replied. "I'm staying in the hotel this time. I have to talk to Ed and let him know what I'm doing."

What *was* he doing? Stephanie didn't dare ask.

Nathan held the cordless telephone to his ear and paced. Hearing Stephanie's voice on the phone was like watching someone eat your favorite flavor of ice cream and not being allowed to have a taste.

"You need to talk to Mr. Phillips?" As Stephanie repeated his words, his heart twisted. She actually sounded worried.

"I'll see you soon, Steph, okay?"

She hesitated for a moment before she answered. "Okay, Nathan. Call me when you get a chance."

They hung up, and then he called Rhonda. "Rhonda, if your plan backfires, it's all your fault."

"Whoa, Nathan. I just made a simple suggestion, that's all. You're a grown man."

"I know. But I have to admit I'm worried."

"Don't worry so much. You'll get lines."

Nathan chuckled out loud. "Lines are something I've never worried about."

"I hate you," she said jokingly. "It's not fair."

"Nothing in life is, Rhonda. It's not fair that you're pulling in more money every year than most families make in ten years."

"But I have nothing to show for it, Nathan," she said sadly. "That's why I told you to take action before it's too late. Commuting won't be too bad if you have someone you love to come home to."

"Okay, I'm doing it."

"Let me know what happens, Nathan."

"Don't worry. You'll be the first I call."

Nathan got off the phone this time and went into high gear. He had two more photo shoots this week before he could leave. But as soon as he was in Hartsville, he had his work really cut out for him. It wouldn't be a picnic talking to Ed, who could be as stubborn as a mule.

Not getting much sleep, Nathan managed to get everything done he needed to do in three days. Next thing he knew he was flying high over land, heading for Hartsville. It was time to take action.

Nathan got off the plane and rented a car in Baker. All during his drive to Hartsville, he thought over and over about what he'd say to both Ed and to Stephanie. Two different discussions, but both very necessary. And neither of them would be easy.

He pulled into the hotel parking lot, got out, and went to the reservations desk to get his room key. Then he unloaded his things into the room so he wouldn't have to do it later, in the dark.

Putting first things first, Nathan called Ed. "Meet me at the Do Drop Inn Diner in about half an hour," he said in as commanding a tone as he could.

"Half an hour?" Ed yelled. "How do you expect me to get there in a half hour?"

"Just do it," Nathan growled.

Then he hopped in and out of the shower and changed clothes. He had so much to do he needed to refresh himself.

Ed was sitting at the diner waiting for him—with Pamela Pritchett sitting across the table from him. He spotted them from outside and groaned. That was what he was trying to avoid.

As soon as he walked inside the place, Pamela squealed his name and moved over against the wall. Ed just sat on the edge, never once taking his eyes off Pamela. They made quite a pair.

With a heavy sigh, Nathan slid into the booth beside Pamela. He glared at Ed and gritted his teeth as he said, "I didn't know you had a date."

"I don't," Ed said appearing filled with self-satisfaction. "I thought you might enjoy seeing our town beauty."

"You and I need to talk, Ed. Just the two of us."

Nathan saw Pamela glance nervously at him out of the corner of his eye. He didn't like what was happening one single bit.

"I'm sorry, Nathan," Pamela said. "I promise I

won't get in the way. The two of you can talk, and I'll just listen."

That wasn't the point. He didn't want her to listen. It was none of her business. But what choice did he have? He sliced a glance her way, then turned his focus back on Ed.

"Okay, have it your way," he said. "I just wanted to let you know that I've decided to move to Harts-ville."

"Ooh," Pamela squealed, reaching out and hugging him. "This is *so* exciting!"

Nathan was so stunned by her sudden action he didn't know what to do when he glanced up and saw Marla and Hank walk in. At first, Marla smiled, but after she saw who was sitting next to him, her look turned into a scowl. Before he had a chance to say anything, she grabbed Hank's arm and led him back out of the diner.

Pamela had Nathan immobilized with her arms around him, and he couldn't get out. He felt helpless.

Ed smiled at Nathan, but it didn't look sincere. In fact, he looked downright panic-stricken. "That's great, Nathan. You'll love it here."

Pamela was grinning from ear to ear, bouncing all over the seat, and making childlike noises. It was too much for Nathan to take at the moment.

"Look, Pamela," he said, glaring at her. "I need to talk to Ed, and I don't want you here."

"Wait a minute," Ed growled at him, his face red

with rage. "That's the woman I love. You can't talk to her like that."

Nathan and Pamela both stopped in their tracks and stared at Ed. "What did you say, Eddie?" she said in a hoarse whisper, unwrapping her arms from around Nathan.

He cleared his throat. A look of embarrassment had taken the place of rage. "I-I'm sorry, Pamela. I hadn't meant for that to come out."

When Nathan turned to look at Pamela, he saw nothing but pure adoration for Ed in her eyes. Well, at least that was settled. Those two were in love and now openly acknowledging it, so they might understand.

He let out a huge sigh and made his own announcement. "Good. I'm in love with Stephanie Mansfield, and I'm going to do everything in my power to make her fall in love with me."

Both heads snapped around and faced Nathan. He sat there and waited for one of them to speak. Finally, Pamela did.

"You love Stephanie?"

"Yes," he replied. "Very much."

"Then we need to get to work," she said. "I've known her all her life. She's pretty dense about matters of the heart since she doesn't have any experience, so I doubt she has any idea how you feel." So Pamela *did* have a heart.

Pamela stood up and tentatively reached for Ed's

hand. He took it, but not before glancing nervously around the diner.

"Hey, Ed, don't worry about what people think. They'll just have to get used to the principal and one of his teachers being in love. I'm sure it happens all the time."

"He what?" Stephanie said through the tears that had instantly formed at the news Marla brought.

"I hate to do this to you, hon," Marla said, reaching out with a tissue, "but I felt like it would be better coming from a friend."

Stephanie nodded and sniffled. "I-I'm glad you did, Marla. It's just that . . ." She couldn't finish her sentence. She'd dared to hope that Nathan might care enough for her to be moving to Hartsville so they could be together. In fact, she even thought there was a chance he might have a future with her in mind.

"Still, though, something seemed off," Marla said as she glanced over at her husband. "Perhaps there was something else going on."

"No, I'm sure you know what you saw, Marla." Stephanie's heart ached with grief of losing something she never really had to begin with. Why would Nathan do something like that to her? They'd spent many weekends getting to know each other, both in New York and in Hartsville. How could she have misread his intentions? Marla was right. Something must have been off.

The sound of more than one car engine outside caused all three of them to turn toward the window. Out in the country like this, any sounds other than nature got her attention.

Hank went over to the front door and opened it. "Well, I'll be."

Mr. Phillips and Pamela Pritchett walked into Stephanie's house hand in hand. Marla crinkled her forehead and cast a curious glance toward Stephanie. Then Nathan walked in right behind them, a huge manila envelope in his hand.

"I finally got the pictures developed," he said. "And what better time than now to take a look."

"It's about time," Marla said, grinning but looking at him funny. "Let's see what kind of damage you did to my ugly mug."

Marla's picture was close to the top. It didn't take long for her to find it. "Not bad," she said as she inspected it. Stephanie could tell she was thrilled to death with the results. Then Marla thumbed through the rest of the pictures and shook her head. "I don't see Steph's."

Mr. Phillips spoke up. "That's because he had so many pictures of her, we had to put them in another envelope."

Marla placed her hands on her hips. "Where are they?"

"In my car," Nathan replied. "I'll take Steph out there later so she can look at them in private."

"But it's dark out there," Pamela said. She looked up at Mr. Phillips, then she nodded and smiled. "Oh."

"Oh, what?" Stephanie asked. "What's going on right now?" Her heart thudded. Something was up; she could tell.

Stephanie looked back and forth between Marla and Hank. Both of them stood there and grinned at her. When she glanced over at Mr. Phillips and Pamela, she saw a similar expression.

Nathan reached out and took her by the hand, calling over his shoulder, "Please excuse us for a few minutes."

Stephanie almost tripped as he pulled her toward his car. He caught her in both arms and dropped a kiss on her forehead. She pulled away.

"Look, Nathan, I don't know—"

He tilted her face up to his, interrupting her. As his face came down over hers, she was helpless to resist his kiss—a long, passionate kiss that sent her senses into orbit.

When he finally pulled away, Stephanie was speechless. "I needed to shut you up while I explain what's going on."

"I—" She couldn't talk. His kiss had done that to her.

"Come here, Stephanie Mansfield," he said as he leaned against his rental car and pulled her against him. "How do you feel about your name being

Stephanie Holloway? Or would you prefer to be Stephanie Mansfield Holloway, either hyphenated or not, that's up to you."

She felt all her blood rush to her toes. Had he just said what she thought he said? He must have because he was standing there waiting for an answer.

Stephanie opened her mouth, but nothing would come out. He'd just have to settle for a big, silly grin.

"Okay, I don't mind if you want to keep your own name. It doesn't matter. But what does matter is that I can be with you for the rest of our lives. I love you, Stephanie, and I want you to be my wife."

She gulped. "Stephanie Holloway is fine."

Nathan scooped her into his arms and kissed her even deeper, more passionately than the last time. She never wanted to come up for air, but she knew they had an audience in the house. She'd seen the light inside go off, meaning they wanted to get a better look.

"How are we going to do this?" she asked. "You live in New York, and I live in Hartsville."

"Well, Rhonda and I talked about it—"

"You discussed this with Rhonda?" she shrieked.

"Sorry, but I needed advice from an expert," he explained. "Anyway, Rhonda told me to ask you what you wanted to do. If you want to stay on your grandmother's property, then we could live here, and I can commute. I'll keep my apartment in New York, and we can spend summers there." He looked down at her with love in his eyes. "That is, if it's all right with you, Stephanie Holloway."

Suddenly, all was right with the world. "Yes, that's fine with me."

Nathan offered the thumbs-up sign toward the house, and the light came on right as everyone inside began to whoop and cheer.

Now, when they kissed, Stephanie was ready for it. And she felt especially good since she'd be able to do this for the rest of her life.

"I love you, Stephanie, and I want to make you happy," he said as he took her hand and walked back toward the house with her by his side.